# A Game of Ponies

BOOK 5

# A Game of Ponies

By Helen Haraldsen

A Game of Ponies



www.helenharaldsen.co.uk



Editing, cover design, and formatting by Let's Get Booked:

www.letsgetbooked.com

Paperback ISBN: 978-1-913953-09-6

eBook ISBN: 978-1-913953-10-2

*This book is dedicated to my grandparents, Elizabeth 'Lizzie' and Thorstein Hammersheim Haraldsen who loved to come and watch me at 'gymkhanos'!*

# Contents

# - One -

## First Impressions

It was the start of the summer holidays, and Amber was looking forward to spending her days at the farm, riding. She could put maths, homework, teachers and some of her fellow students to the back of her mind for six weeks. Instead, she'd hack in the forestry with JoJo, go to shows at the weekends with Molly, and possibly with Honey too, once her sore eye was fully healed. She also hoped to spend some time with Caroline, the farmer's grown-up daughter, having more lessons with Molly. Caroline had already helped her so much, and Amber looked up to her like a big sister. She was so patient, quiet and gentle, and had such a deep understanding of horses and how to get the best out of them. Amber wanted to be just like her. She wondered if she'd be able to help Caroline with her new horse, Lady, as she was preparing the ex-racehorse for a new career as an event horse. Being helpful to Caroline was a fantasy she often played out in her head. Amber spent many happy hours daydreaming about ways in which she could impress Caroline.

It was during one of these daydreams at breakfast that her father made an announcement.

"Well, we'd better get ready and head to the farm," he said. "I've arranged for a chap I work with to bring his daughter to meet Pearl at ten o'clock. He doesn't know where the farm is, so I've told him we'll meet him in the bypass layby, and he can follow us from there."

Amber snapped her head up from her cereal to look at her dad. "What? Who's coming to see Pearl? Why?"

Mr Anderson gulped the last of his tea and took his mug to the sink to wash it. He tried to look over his shoulder to speak to Amber at the same time and ended up getting water all over his T-shirt. As he dabbed at it with a tea towel, he explained. "Someone I work with, Bill, has a daughter who's been having riding lessons. She'd like a pony of her own, but Bill and his wife aren't horsey." He gave up with the towel and decided he'd have to change his T-shirt. He folded the towel and placed it on the cold radiator. "They're thinking of getting her a pony, but before they do, they want her to learn a bit more about looking after one. I think he also wants to see if she's still keen when she has to do the work herself, rather than just turning up to ride with the pony ready to go. I said she could come up to the farm over the holidays and do a bit with Pearl. She can ride her and help with mucking out and tack cleaning."

"And you didn't think to mention until now that you've told him his daughter could come and be babysat by me for the summer?" Amber asked, her voice dripping with sarcasm.

"It'll be good company for you," he added hopefully.

"And this is starting *today*?" Amber asked, her left eyebrow raised. She would never be able to pull off a poker face as that eyebrow always arched of its own accord when she was unimpressed by something.

"Er, yeah."

"How old is she?"

"Erm, I'm not sure. Nine or ten, maybe? Still in primary school."

Amber didn't reply, but Mr Anderson noticed her jaw clench as if she was biting back words of disapproval.

"I'll just go and change this T-shirt," he said, seeing a chance to escape. "Get yourself ready. We need to leave in the next five minutes."

*Great,* thought Amber. *A nine-year-old is practically a baby.* She was only thirteen herself, but she felt like she'd grown up a lot lately, and a nine-year-old seemed so young to her. She wanted to spend her summer at the farm either with Caroline or JoJo and seethed that her father had volunteered to take on this kid they'd never even met. She might be a complete pain. *Then again,* Amber thought, *she might look up to me. JoJo apparently thinks I'm inspiring, so I could be, like, a role model. It could be like having a little sister.* Amber imagined this little girl admiring her as she admired Caroline. As an only child, she wondered what that might feel like.

*I'll just have to hope she's nice. Everyone has to start somewhere.* Amber rinsed her bowl and went up to the bathroom to clean her teeth and check her hair. She also changed her T-shirt and put on one of her favourites: a maroon polo shirt with little foxes on it, instead of the plain grey one she had been wearing. If this girl was going to be her protégé, Amber wanted to make a good first impression.

All the way to the farm, Amber imagined what the girl would be like. She was Georgina, Georgia, or Georgie, according to Mr Anderson, who could never remember people's names and called everyone 'thingy'. Amber decided that she'd be timid and unassuming and would need some nurturing to bring her out of her shell. Amber would be able to impart all the wisdom she'd picked up over the last three years, and the girl would come to worship her. They'd end up as lifelong friends and would attend each other's weddings and all that adult stuff when they grew up.

***

They pulled into the farm yard and parked in their usual spot, with her dad's friend placing his car right behind theirs. Doors opened and clunked shut as the car occupants climbed out and regarded each other.

"Bill!" Mr Anderson stepped forward and shook the other man's hand as if he'd just met him. He pumped the hand vigorously, making Bill almost topple forward on top of him.

"Andrew," he replied, "and you must be Amber," he acknowledged her, and she nodded. "I've heard so much about you. And this is…"

"Hi, I'm Georgia. Pleased to meet you." The girl stepped forward and offered her hand to Mr Anderson, then Amber, with such precocious confidence it made Amber purse her lips.

"Er, yes, you too," Mr Anderson also seemed taken aback by Georgia's confidence. As he'd said, she couldn't have been older than nine or ten, and she'd never met them before, but she immediately took charge of the situation.

"I'm here to see your ponies," Georgia informed him. "Where are they?" She looked around the farm yard as if she expected to see them all ready and tacked up, waiting for her.

"They're in the field. We'll get some head collars and go and get them." Mr Anderson headed towards their tack room, and everyone followed. "Have you caught a pony before, Georgina?"

"Georgia. No, I haven't. Are they very far away?"

"Just in this field here." Mr Anderson indicated a gate to the right of the tack room. "I'll just get those head collars."

Amber observed Georgia quietly as they all traipsed into the field and crossed the little stream in the dip. She was rattling on about all the different ponies she'd ridden at the riding school she went to. She talked non-stop about them: their names, colours, which one had the nicest trot, which one was scared of umbrellas, which one could take a polo mint from between a person's lips so gently you didn't feel it. It was like someone had pressed a 'play' button, and she would constantly talk until someone pressed 'stop'. Amber sighed, but no-one appeared to notice, and she was free to appraise Georgia from behind as she kept to the back of the group.

Apart from negotiating the stream somewhat tentatively, not wanting to get mud on her boots, Georgia walked with big long strides, her dark brown bob bouncing and her back as straight as a new pencil. She was wearing a mint green Joules top and beige jodhpurs. No-one wore beige jodhpurs unless they were going to a show or to a riding school where they wouldn't get dirty as they wouldn't have to do anything. This kid looked ready to model for an equestrian catalogue rather than catch and groom a muddy Fell pony. Amber trailed along after them, wishing that her dad had kept his mouth shut and not invited Bill to bring his daughter along for the day.

"There they are." Mr Anderson pointed as they reached the top of an incline and saw the ponies standing together nearby. "The chestnut there is Molly, and the black ones are our Fell ponies, Honey and Pearl. Let's get these on them and bring them in."

Mr Anderson gave Amber two of the head collars before walking over to Molly to put hers on. For some reason, Honey was often reluctant to be caught by him, so Amber was responsible for getting her. Before she did so, she showed Georgia how to hold Pearl's head collar and slip it on her face. Georgia watched Amber do it, then took a turn herself, managing the task easily.

Amber left Georgia holding Pearl as she went to get Honey.

"Oh, she's so lovely," the girl exclaimed, eyes wide with adoration as she pulled her fingers gently through Pearl's long black mane. Amber smiled warily at Georgia as she led Honey up beside her. The way the girl looked at Pearl, taking in every inch of her as if she was recently discovered treasure, reminded Amber of how she'd once looked at the pony in the same way. But not so much recently. Her first pony, the one she'd loved so much, had been overlooked as she'd battled to build her relationship with Molly. So much of her focus had been on the new pony and the tetrathlon competitions she'd done that year; it had left little room for anything else. Apart from riding Pearl in a recent treasure hunt, she'd hardly had any time for her pony. The corners of her smile wavered as Amber realised she'd been ignoring Pearl for months and a shroud of guilt settled on her shoulders.

The girl continued to praise Pearl as she stroked her lovingly all her way back across the field towards the stables and told her father what a beautiful pony she was.

"Yes, isn't she?" Bill agreed. "Isn't it nice of Amber to let you come and ride her?" He looked across at Amber, and she smiled back politely. She was aware she'd hardly uttered a word to their visitors, and she dropped her head, pretending to adjust Honey's fly mask. Her smile wavered as her insides twisted. With everything else that had been going on recently, Amber knew she hadn't given Pearl much attention over the last few months. But she was still *her* Pearl. And now, here was this girl, who was nothing like Amber had imagined, or hoped, come to take over her for the summer.

*Why do I feel like this?* Amber wondered, noticing the dread that was settling itself inside her like an unwelcome visitor. *Am I jealous?* She narrowed her eyes, hoping this was not the case. *No, that's not it. It's her. Her manner. Her attitude. She seems too full of herself. I get the feeling she's not going to be interested in Pearl for long.*

This idea both cheered and saddened Amber at the same time. If she could get rid of Georgia as soon as possible, she'd be free to spend her time at the farm with Caroline or JoJo, which was what she wanted. But… her protectiveness of Pearl meant that she didn't want the pony to be dismissed or criticised. She knew all about Pearl's faults, and she definitely wasn't a perfect pony, but she was perfect in her own way. Ever since Amber's brief period of misjudging Pearl's worth, she'd vowed never to compare her to other ponies or to undervalue her again. And she wasn't going to let anyone else do so either. She hadn't spoken up when Elisha Templeton said nasty things about Pearl, but she would now.

*Be careful,* the voice in her head warned her. *You might be misjudging Georgia.*

*Yes, I know,* Amber told it. *But I'm on my guard with her. I just get a feeling about her that I don't like. That's my first impression.*

*Wait and see,* the voice warned her.

*Yes, we'll see.*

# - Two -

# Amber's Sacrifice

"So, how'd it go?" Mrs Anderson asked over tea later that day. She'd been at work and hadn't been able to come to the farm to meet Georgia.

Amber chewed carefully on her chicken, thinking about how to answer the question. She didn't want to sound nasty and knew she needed to choose her words carefully. She looked to her dad to see if he might answer, but apparently, he had a mouth full of chicken too and couldn't speak.

"Er… well… Georgia was… *interesting.*"

"Hmmm, *interesting,* eh? How so?" Mrs Anderson smirked as she speared a piece of broccoli, recognising Amber's attempt to be tactful.

"She wasn't what I was expecting," Amber said, launching into a description of what happened when they brought the ponies in from the field.

Georgia had shown great interest in learning how to groom – something she hadn't done before – and would've spent all day brushing Pearl if Amber hadn't said they'd better tack up and go for a ride. Honey still couldn't be ridden as her eye wasn't fully healed, so Amber demonstrated how to saddle and bridle Molly so that everything was comfortable for the pony, and then helped Georgia to put Pearl's tack on. Georgia was a good student, and when Amber checked Pearl over, she was pleased to see that everything was as it should be. She congratulated Georgia for doing so well, which the younger girl seemed to appreciate. Amber started to relax, thinking that perhaps she'd been too quick to judge Georgia, and maybe she was alright after all.

But then they'd gone for a short hack out, their dads following behind with Kasper, the cocker spaniel. Amber noticed that Georgia's position was very upright and stiff. She held her reins tightly and too short, pulling the bit up into the corners of Pearl's mouth. Thinking this was down to nerves, which Amber fully sympathised with, she gently tried to reassure her.

"Georgia, I know it's strange riding a pony you're not used to for the first time, but you can relax with Pearl. She's well behaved and won't do anything naughty. You can loosen your reins a bit – don't be nervous."

"I'm *not* nervous," Georgia replied indignantly. "This is how I've been taught to ride. My instructor says too many riders slouch about and don't pay proper attention when they're riding, which could cause an accident if the pony shies at something. I'm being *alert*."

"Okay," Amber replied, thinking that Georgia was taking her instructor's words a tad too literally. "Alert is definitely good, but you could just give Pearl a bit of slack in the reins, so the bit isn't up against the bars of her mouth. I don't think that's comfortable for her."

"If I do that and she shies at something, I could fall off."

Amber took a deep breath. "You can't use the pony's mouth to hang onto for balance, though," she pointed out. "Ponies need to be able to move their heads to see things properly. A really tight contact can restrict their vision and make them shy because they can't see things clearly. You could try leaning forward slightly – just bring your shoulders forward a bit more, then if she does stumble or shy, you won't lose your balance and pull on her mouth."

"My instructor says—"

"And that's how it was the whole way round," Amber told her mother. "Whenever I tried to tell her something, she wouldn't listen. I just got '*my instructor says*' to everything I suggested. Poor Pearl had to go the whole way with her hanging onto her mouth for grim death. She was hard work. I cut the ride short and didn't go as far as I planned. I just wanted to get back and get her off Pearl. She's not coming again, is she?" She looked at Mr Anderson, who put his cutlery down onto his plate and sighed.

"I had a talk with her dad while we were walking the dog," he said, "and I think he'd really appreciate it if you let her come again. He knows she can be a bit… difficult. Georgia hasn't got any friends at school as she isn't interested in the things they like. She's one of those kids who's nine going on thirty. He thought, as you're older, you could become a bit of a friend for her?"

"Oh, no pressure then. I've been 'selected' to be her friend. Lucky me. She's a pain though!"

"Well, maybe, but she's just a kid, Amber. Maybe she *was* a bit anxious but didn't want to let on. She might be better when she gets to know you. Look at Caroline. She never used to speak, but now she's like a different person."

"Well, Georgia has no trouble speaking; she never shuts up," Amber pointed out. "It'd have to work the opposite way with her – the more she gets to know you, the less she talks?"

"Perhaps. She could talk too much out of nervousness. Let her come again and see how it goes?" Mr Anderson looked hopefully at his daughter.

Amber sighed. She didn't have many friends at school either and found people her own age a bit baffling. The way they all seemed to be obsessed with boys and make-up, and shopping made her feel left out. All she wanted to talk about was ponies, but nobody else at school shared her interest. That's why it was so good that she now had JoJo, Emily and Chelsea, who did. And the fact that they were all more confident than her helped. Whenever she was with them or spoke to them, even just through messages, their confidence seemed to transfer to her like osmosis. Where would she be without them? Would she still be the shy, socially awkward person she was deep down? They'd helped her to see she had qualities that others admired. They'd helped her to start to accept herself and like herself more. Amber knew that if she had the chance to help Georgia in the way her friends had helped her, she should, but despite this, she pulled a face and whined, "Oh, Daaaaad."

Mr Anderson stood up and started stacking their dishes. Kasper jumped up expectantly, hoping there were some scraps left for him. "I'll give Bill a ring and see what Georgia thought of today. She might not want to come back. But if she does, I think it'd be nice if you gave her another chance." He looked at her pointedly, making her feel guilty and obliged at the same time.

"Oh, I suppose so," she huffed, hoping to convey how much effort it took to be noble and self-sacrificing. "But don't get your hopes up. I don't think me and Georgia are going to end up being BFF's."

# - Three -

## Sibling Rivalry

It turned out that Georgia had *loved* her visit to the farm. According to her dad, she hadn't stopped talking about how wonderful Pearl was and how she liked that Amber wasn't slapdash in the way she tacked up the ponies. She'd loved the way Amber took such care to ensure everything was comfortable for the ponies, with no hair or skin trapped that could pinch them. Apparently, he and his wife had heard a lot of 'Amber says', since the visit. She'd love to come back again, but they were going to visit some family for the next week and wanted to come when they returned.

"Well," said Amber, her left eyebrow arching, "I'd never have believed that. She didn't give me any impression that she liked me at all."

"It seems she did, though, so I've told Bill she can definitely come back again," Mr Anderson said as he locked the back door.

They were heading to Shaw Farm. Amber was looking forward to it. She had arranged to go to JoJo's on Molly to practise some Pony Club Games. Since Matthew, JoJo's little brother, had started riding her old pony, Flash, he'd developed a love of it. It appeared to have overtaken his interest in tetrathlon, and now he was determined to be chosen for the club's Area Games team the following year. He had the Prince Philip Cup in his sights, and Amber had been summoned to make up numbers in their at-home training.

Riding the short distance from the farm to JoJo's house, Amber enjoyed a brief return to her daydream of being idolised by Georgia. Imagining the girl at home telling her parents all about what 'Amber says' made her smile. By the time she arrived at JoJo's gate, she felt like she could do anything.

"Hiya!" JoJo greeted her as she led her pale palomino, Merry, out of the stable. "I hope you're ready for this. Matty is taking this *super serious* and is determined to beat us both, so that means we have to make sure he doesn't."

Amber laughed at the competitive nature the two siblings shared. She knew they both really would be going all-out to beat each other. She was just there to have fun. Amber knew she wouldn't win - not with JoJo there - but she said, "I'll do my best."

The girls rode into the schooling paddock to warm up while they waited for Matthew to make his grand entrance. The show jumps had been pushed into corners, and the poles lay along the fence line to keep them out of the way. The centre of the paddock had been set up with three lanes of bending poles: traffic cones with garden canes protruding out of them. An assortment of plastic mugs topped some of the poles in each lane: one lane had green mugs, one yellow and one red. Tubs of flags waited at the edge of the paddock. These were also made from garden canes and old tea towels. It made Amber smile to see how everything was laid out so correctly, with the poles set at the correct distance and the colour-coded mugs for each lane. Even though the equipment was decidedly homemade, it didn't stop Matthew from being meticulous about the details. Most boys she knew had a may-care, *it'll do* attitude, but Matthew was developing into something of a perfectionist now that he'd found something he wanted to focus on. It was an attitude shared by his sister, who would soon be heading to the Tethrathlon Championships and had her sights set on making it into the North of England Tetrathlon team next year. Their ambition was lost on Amber. She wanted to develop as a rider as much as possible, but she knew she wasn't capable of brilliance. Plus, she wasn't interested in the stress, focus and discipline required to get to the top of a sport. She was quite happy doing a bit of everything.

"Okay, girls, prepare to take on the boys," Matthew called as he burst through the gate on Flash.

The pony was on form. He'd had a good long break since his accident with JoJo and now looked fighting fit again. He pranced into the paddock sideways, tossing his head, and Amber marvelled at how Matthew sat astride him, looking completely relaxed. Only recently, he'd been on his super-steady Sam, but had managed to transition seamlessly, just like Natalie Riley, to a pony as far at the other end of the spectrum as it was possible to be. The thought made Amber's 'I-can-do-anything' attitude from moments earlier wither slightly as she considered that here was another rider who had gone from a quiet first pony to a super-charged competition pony without batting an eyelid. She was still getting used to the massive difference between the Fell ponies and Molly. *Why has it been such a struggle for me but not them?*

Amber also noted that Flash was bitted in a snaffle as that was the only one permitted for Pony Club Games.

*How's he going to manage to steer and stop him in that?* Amber wondered, thinking back to how semi-uncontrollable Flash used to be when JoJo rode him, even when bitted up and strapped down with all sorts of curbs and nosebands.

"Oh no, boyos. *Here come the girls.*" JoJo sang, pointing at herself and Amber, both mounted on mares. "We're gonna walk all up and down your ass!"

"Er, Jo. Language, please." Mr Jones strolled into the paddock carrying a cup of tea. He plonked himself in a plastic garden chair, ready to be their starter.

"Sorry, Dad," JoJo called, "but Matty's being a menace again."

"Shut up, Joey," he retaliated.

"Don't call me Joey, you little—"

"RIGHT! Come on, get ready to start. I see Matty's set it up so that you can race each other. Another time we'll have you all taking turns on one line of poles so you can practise hand overs." Mr Jones pointed vaguely at an imaginary start line. "And thank you, Amber, for coming to provide my very *grateful* son with some competition. May the best man…or woman, win. Now, get on the start line, and we'll do the bending race first."

The three riders lined their ponies up with a row of poles while Mr Jones remained in his seat, holding up one of the tea towel flags. Amber watched him carefully, waiting for the flag to drop, signalling the start of the race, trying to avoid being distracted by Flash, who was rearing on the start line, impatient for the signal to go.

The flag fell.

"Go on!" Amber urged Molly, suddenly gripped by a surge of excitement.

Molly shot forward, and they weaved around the flags easily, but not fast enough to beat JoJo and Merry, whose turn around the end pole was brilliant.

"Loser!" JoJo called as Matthew and Flash charged over the finish line in last place. Matthew's scowl was plain to see even though his riding hat covered the frown lines rippling his forehead.

"Shut up. It's only cos Flash was rearing and didn't see the flag drop – he set off after you two. It's the only one you'll win!"

He was wrong. They lined up twice more, but Flash was always too excited to settle as he waited for the signal to start, and JoJo won both races. Amber had to be content with her second place in the bending race as Matthew beat her in the two flag and then the mug race. This seemed to placate him slightly, but Amber pitied him a sister like JoJo. He was clearly desperate to beat her, but JoJo was someone who could win without even looking like she was trying. She didn't have one specialist area either; no, she was one of those people who seemed to be good at everything. Amber wondered what that must be like. She was barely 'good' at anything. She'd love to discover something that could be 'her thing'.

When Amber was younger, before ponies, she'd tried music but found that playing musical instruments wasn't her thing either. The violin and piano had both been started and dropped. She couldn't sing. She was too shy for acting. Sports involving coordination were out.

Amber had hoped that riding would be her thing, but although she enjoyed it, she knew she didn't have the natural talent of people like JoJo. It was hard to be her friend at times, as resentment often tried to grow between them like a vicious bramble. Amber had to snap it off before it grew too strong and took hold, like the choking weed it was. It wasn't JoJo's fault she was so good at everything. It wasn't like she looked down on Amber. In fact, JoJo had told her that she was *inspiring*. Amber often thought about the moment she'd said it and clung to it like a life belt. The idea that you could still be admired without being 'the best' was something new to her, and she had to keep reminding herself of it, letting it settle in and take root so that it could grow and flower.

"Okay, you lot, last race." Mr Jones had placed a feed bucket in the middle of each of their lanes with three pairs of rolled-up socks at the end. "Come on, Flash, you plonker. Put your front feet on the ground and stop being a gremlin." He shook his head at the chestnut pony, who knew another race was about to begin and was doing an impression of a rocking horse, as usual. It was amazing, Amber thought, how both JoJo and Matthew had this competitive drive even though their parents were totally laid back, while Emily had none, despite having a super-competitive father. She knew that Matthew would be desperate to win this one and get the final victory over his sister, but Flash would make it difficult. Merry, on the other hand, though she was eager to start too – poised and ready to launch as soon as the flag fell - remained still, waiting for the signal. Even Molly, after three races, felt buzzed. She pawed the ground with a front foot as Amber held her back.

"Go!" Mr Jones dropped the flag. The three flew to the end of their lane, where each dropped from their pony and collected a sock. Flash and Merry were away in a gallop immediately, understanding what was expected of them, while their riders vaulted on before pulling them up at the feed bucket to drop the sock in, turning the ponies back to the pile for the next one. They were neck and neck.

Amber was stuck. Despite all the work she'd done with Molly at getting her to stand still for mounting, this was proving far too exciting for the pony. There was no way Amber had the confidence to attempt to vault on to a galloping pony, so she needed to remount. But seeing the other two ponies hurtling away from her was too much for Molly. Every time Amber attempted to put her foot in the stirrup, Molly went to shoot forward. Not wanting to undo all the good work she'd been doing with Caroline to get Molly to relax and stand still to be mounted, she dropped her sock and gave up trying to get back on Molly. She pulled the fractious pony towards her and tried to settle her, but by now, JoJo and Matthew had finished their race and were at the other end of the field. Amber walked towards them, Molly dancing beside her as Amber held the reins close to her chin.

"Who won?" she called.

"Me!" Both of their voices carried towards her, still racing to get there first.

"It was a draw." Mr Jones sighed. "Are you okay, Amber?"

"Oh yeah, she just got a bit overexcited, and I couldn't get back on. I don't want to end up with another broken collarbone, so we've called it a day. I don't think games is our thing, is it, girl?" She stroked Molly's white nose and loosened her grip on the reins, now that they were back with the others.

"Do you wanna come for a short hack with us now to cool them off?" JoJo asked.

Amber glanced over at her friend and laughed. She was sitting back-to-front on Merry – JoJo's beaming face and Merry's vanilla coloured tail looked back at her.

"Yeah, why not?" That familiar feeling of failure had just been starting to nibble at Amber's insides, threatening to eat away at her good mood, but JoJo and her silliness saved the day. Amber pushed the feeling away, leading Molly back into the yard to remount while JoJo swivelled herself back around in the saddle so that she was facing forwards again.

"You coming, loser?" JoJo asked her brother.

"I won that last race, JOEY."

"No, you didn't."

"Yes, I did."

Amber sighed and relaxed in the saddle as they rode through the gate onto the farm track, the two siblings bickering all the way.

# - Four -

# Nemesis

Sunday was show day. Or at least, show jumping day. Highland Park Equestrian Centre was running a summer show jumping points league in their new and enormous outdoor arena, and everyone wanted to go. Even riders from Scotland and the North East would travel over for the unaffiliated competition that now looked and felt like an Olympic venue

Amber had seen pictures of the new arena online, but this was her first time riding in it. When her eyes landed on the statues of two pale marble lions facing each other at the entrance to the pristine arena, her mind boggled. She'd seen pictures of them on the centre's website, but the real thing gave her goosebumps. The snarling faces of the life-sized lions towered over her as they sat on their pedestals like reigning kings. They weren't exactly welcoming. Amber gulped, wondering what Molly would make of them. At least she hadn't brought Honey today; she would probably need to be blindfolded to get her past them.

"Boo! What are you entering?" Amber squealed as she felt something sharp jab her in the ribs and shout in her ear at the same time.

Emily. Who else?

"Jeez! Do you have to do that? These lions are scary enough without you actually pouncing on me and roaring like that. Are you trying to kill me?"

Emily arranged her hands to resemble claws in front of her and launched into the chorus of the Katy Perry song, *Roar*. Amber cringed as she noticed some people nearby smirking as they witnessed Emily's performance.

"Will you shut up, you idiot? You're such an embarrassment." She pushed her away, trying to suppress a smile but failing.

"Ahh, you love it, really," Emily put her hands on her hips and repeated her question, "so…which classes are you doing? You can do two."

“Erm… what have you entered?” Amber asked, trying to look nonchalant. She would go for 75cm and 85cm if it were up to her, but she didn’t want to be jumping smaller than her friends. She knew that JoJo wasn’t here as Merry wasn’t a great show jumper, and she was preparing for the Tetrathlon Championships taking place next week, but Chelsea was coming to do the 95cm and 105cm. She was now competing at BE100 with Skylark, an ex-showjumper who had no problem doing the top classes. And what about Emily?

“Harry’s here with me today. He’s done the 55cm and will be doing the 65cm any minute.” She glanced over her shoulder at the nearby collecting ring. Amber followed her gaze and saw Emily’s little brother on Fudge, warming up over the practice fence. Mr Pryde appeared to be coaching him enthusiastically, even though he didn’t actually ride himself. “I’ve left them to it for a minute. Dad’s doing my head in. I think the grandeur’s got to him.” She swept an arm to indicate the gleaming show jumps, all perfectly presented on the sand and encased in white post and rail fencing. “He thinks he’s at the European Championships or something. I wish he’d chill out and just enjoy it. And let *us* enjoy it," she added under her breath.

"So…what…?" Amber went to ask, for the second time.

"Oh, yeah… sorry. I'm doing 85 and 95cm. Dad wants me doing the 95 and 105, of course, but I've pointed out we'll probably be here 'til 8pm if we stay for the last class as there are millions here. We got here at 9am for Harry to do the 55cm, and the classes are huge. They're still only on the 65cm now. It's going to be a long day."

The girls placed their entries, Amber opting for the same classes Emily entered, and hung around the edge of the arena watching the riders in the 65cm class, waiting for Harry to take his turn on Fudge. Soon, he came trotting in, the loudspeaker announcing the arrival of Harry Pryde and Freaky Treacle. Emily squeaked and clasped her hands together as the whistle blew, and Harry rode Fudge at the first fence.

"Good boy," Emily whispered as Fudge popped over number one and carried on to the next fence. Amber was aware of Emily's body bobbing next to her as she rode every fence with her little brother. Even Amber found her eyes welling up as she watched Fudge taking such good care of his new, novice rider. It looked like he would get a clear round until Fudge got too close to the plank fence and tipped the top plank off with a front hoof.

"And that's four faults for Harry and Freaky Treacle," the loudspeaker blared.

"Urrghh," Emily moaned, her body slumping like a flat tyre.

"That was good," Amber said, knowing that Harry hadn't been riding long and was just starting to do jumping. "He did so well." She didn't add that he'd be kicking himself for having the last fence down. She'd had that experience herself when she'd relaxed at the final fence, thinking a clear round was in the bag. She wouldn't make that mistake ever again, and neither would Harry. It was a lesson learned.

"It won't be good enough for Dad." Emily straightened herself back up as she watched Harry ride out of the arena to be greeted by a stern-faced Mr Pryde. "I'd better go and rescue him. See you in a bit?" Amber nodded as Emily ran towards her brother. She smiled, watching as Emily patted Fudge and beamed up at Harry, clearly telling him how well he'd done. But smiles quickly faded as Mr Pryde and Emily appeared to be arguing. Amber couldn't hear the words being said from where she stood, but she could see from the faces that no-one was happy. Mr Pryde was pointing into the arena at the plank fence, which had been put back up, ready for the next rider. Emily was shaking her head, both of them mouthing words that somehow looked ugly, even though they couldn't be heard. Not wanting to hear any more, Emily grabbed Fudge's reins and pulled him around, leading him away from her father. Amber lost sight of her as they weaved their way through the mass of ponies in the collecting ring and disappeared from view.

Watching this little scene made Amber feel uncomfortable. Her parents didn't put any pressure on her at shows, which was just as well as she put enough on herself. If Amber made a mistake, their reaction was 'never mind'. They knew that she *so* wanted to do well, and when mistakes happened, she was so disappointed in herself, she didn't need them to add to it. Why didn't Mr Pryde get that? Why couldn't he accept that every round can't be perfect? Did he think riders made mistakes on purpose? Did he understand that ponies can make mistakes? Did he see that every round is a learning experience, and there's no point assigning blame when things go wrong? It's one thing to point out if a rider is doing something that isn't helping the pony to jump well, to help them understand what they can do to improve, but it didn't look like Mr Pryde was doing that. He didn't even know how to ride. He had no idea how difficult it was. She'd have liked to point this out to him, but didn't dare. She could imagine how he'd take her advice.

The thought that Emily and Harry had to live with constant expectation and criticism made Amber's insides twitch. The sound of the loudspeaker announcing all the riders and their faults, the hot sun beating down on her and the smell of bacon and onions cooking nearby added to the sense of nausea growing inside her. She returned to the trailer park and hurried inside her own trailer, where she breathed in the smell of hay and stroked Molly's neck in an attempt to smooth out the knots growing inside her. *Why do I always feel like this at shows?* She wondered. *I'm here because I want to be, so why do I always feel like I'm going to be sick?*

Walking the course for the 85cm class didn't make her feel any better. This was only her first class, with a bigger one still to come, yet the fences looked huge. And wide. And scary. There was a water tray, a skinny stile, a gate, and several sets of scary fillers. One fence even had postbox wings with fillers beneath in the form of addressed envelopes complete with stamps. These were topped with red and white poles. The whole course looked super professional and exciting to ride. That's what Amber told herself as she moved from fence to fence, Emily back beside her. *I'm not nervous. I'm excited.*

The collecting ring was busy, and the girls didn't get much of a chance to chat as they warmed their ponies up. Pink was being her usual self – crab stepping and cantering sideways, making Emily have to work hard to stop her crashing into the other riders.

"Let her go!" Mr Pryde shouted at Emily as she kept the pony on a tight rein to stop her racing up behind the pony she was following into a practice fence.

"Yeah, great advice, Dad," Amber heard her mutter as she ignored him. Her usually soft, bright face looked stern and tense. It was like she was a different person when her dad was around.

Amber wished Emily would be her usual funny, silly self as she could normally always be relied on to lift Amber's spirits when she was feeling tense. But then Amber heard something that totally distracted her.

"And now in the ring, we have Elisha Templeton and Lady Bluebell."

Emily had obviously heard it too, as both girls rode nearer the main arena where they could see Elisha just beginning her round on a beautiful dapple-grey pony. It jumped the first fence well but let out a huge buck on landing. Elisha yanked the pony's head up and booted it towards the next jump.

"What's she doing here? And what's that pony? She rides horses now!"

"I don't know, but I'll find out." Emily whisked her phone out of her jacket pocket and hurriedly started tapping the screen.

"Amber Anderson? You're next to go," the steward told her, glancing up at Amber from her clipboard.

Elisha had a difficult round on Lady Bluebell, who bucked and plunged all the way, but somehow she managed to stay clear. As she rode out of the arena, passing right next to Amber, Elisha's eyes slid across towards her. Recognition sparked between them like a snap of electricity.

"And now we have Amber Anderson riding Just Molly," the loudspeaker announced, followed immediately by the sharp blast of a whistle.

But seeing Elisha, knowing that she was here and would probably be watching her round, made Amber feel like trapped prey with a predator waiting to pounce on her. Her breath quickened, and her muscles tightened.

Molly heard the starting whistle and felt her rider's reaction. She responded automatically, striking off into a canter and waiting to be directed towards the first fence. Where was it? Why wasn't Amber telling her which way to go? Molly flicked her ears back uncertainly, asking her rider for instructions. But Amber couldn't tell her. She couldn't remember where the first fence was. All she could think was *Elisha's here.* There was no room for anything else.

An army of thoughts raided Amber's mind, leaving no room to think about where she was or what she should be doing. Elisha's past words trooped out of a part of her mind where she'd been keeping them locked up and at bay since she'd last seen her a year ago. They lined up, ready to torment her.

"As if she could be in this group on *that*…fancy getting eliminated over jumps as small as those, how pathetic is *that*…she'll spoil the day on that tortoise…fat little hair-balls…pathetic second-rate ponies." They stung like slaps, especially as each one was paired with the memory of how Elisha had looked at Honey and Pearl.

The words. The looks. So real, so raw. Amber winced. She couldn't do this.

Another memory jumped in: Elisha seeing her with Molly at their first show. "You've been in the little classes? What an insult to Molly. You're not riding your no-hope Fell pony anymore," and, "You won a 70cm class? Well done, you'll be at the Olympics next." But right on its heels, another memory followed after it: Elisha being eliminated at the Pony Club camp event while Amber came third on her 'no-hope Fell pony' and beat her. And riding on this came the final memory of her clear round at the tough Area Tetrathlon competition on Molly just a week ago. *I* can *do this. I'll show her.*

Forcing all her thoughts back into their box and cramming the lid on to silence them, she looked frantically around the arena. If she didn't start soon, her time would run out, and she'd be eliminated without even presenting at a fence. Amber couldn't let that happen.

She spotted the first fence and quickly steered Molly towards it.

"Sorry, girl," she apologised as Molly had to adjust herself to clear the first jump on the course. Amber hadn't had time to establish a good rhythm as she rushed to start within the time allowed, and now she pulled Molly back to a trot, restarting the canter on the correct lead before bearing right for the second fence – a straightforward yellow and white upright. Molly cleared it easily but didn't feel like she was moving forward enough to take on the next fence: an ascending oxer.

Amber put her leg on and gave Molly a small tap on the shoulder with her whip. The pony picked up and left the poles untouched, but Amber had to work at every fence. Molly struggled through the double, getting a stride and a shuffle in, where it should have been one easy stride for her, resulting in a pole off the second part. Amber ignored it, focussing on the final fence – the planks. It was on a slight dog-leg, and she knew she needed to keep her right leg on to stop Molly drifting past it as she'd seen some other ponies do. Molly stayed straight and cleared the planks without touching them.

"Phew," she said as she left the arena, patting Molly. Four faults was a shame, but she wouldn't have been bothered by it if she'd felt that Molly had jumped well. With the next, bigger round still to come, it would've been nice for that round to go well and give her confidence. But Molly had felt reluctant. After the way she'd flown round the huge Area Tetrathlon cross-country course, Amber had expected her to be livelier today. She put it down to the distraction at the start of the round and the way it had made her lose concentration. Amber wouldn't do that in the next round.

Another rider passed her as she left the arena, and was soon announced as Marcus Winter, riding Polar Bear. *Their names are well-matched,* she thought before she noticed Emily waiting to go next, circling Pink just outside the entrance.

"Amber!" she called, waving her over with one hand while keeping Pink turning with the other. "I'm in next," she said, "but there's some news about Elisha. Chelsea will tell you."

That was when Amber noticed Chelsea standing on the other side of the rails, probably waiting for her chance to walk the course before her class started.

A clatter came from the arena, and Polar Bear galloped back into the collecting ring, riderless, with reins and stirrups flying. He nearly trampled the steward as he flew through the warm-up area, disappearing into the car park.

"Um, Emily?" The steward picked up the clipboard she'd dropped and pushed her sunglasses back up her nose. "You'd better go in. It looks like that round is finished."

Pink fired herself into the arena, leaving Amber to speak to Chelsea.

"How was your round?" Chelsea asked, reaching through the rails to give Molly a polo mint.

"Oh, not bad. Molly didn't feel great and had one down, but I think it was just because I was distracted."

Amber slid off her pony and loosened the girth. She led her into the shade provided by the indoor arena's shadow and unbuttoned her show jacket. She was almost surprised that no steam escaped through the opened front.

"Yeah, Emily said it was a bit of a shock to see a certain someone here. Last we heard, she was off winning everything on that new horse, Danger Mouse."

"It was," Amber agreed, wishing she could get a drink of water but wanting to find out what Chelsea knew even more. "Emily said you'd tell me about it?"

"Well, I've heard the news about three times removed, so it's hard to know what's true and what's Chinese whispers, but…it seems like the Templetons have had a bit of a fall from grace."

Amber frowned, and Chelsea came closer to her, looking around and lowering her voice.

"Look, I don't like to gossip, but what I've heard is that Elisha's dad has gone bust or something. Anyway, he's lost all his money and took off! He's gone, and by all accounts, no-one knows where. He's sold both of Elisha's horses, that enormous lorry they had, and just left. Mrs Templeton is said to be frantic about it as she doesn't work and doesn't know what they'll do about the mortgage on that massive house they live in, plus she's got Troy, Elisha's waste-of-space brother to worry about."

"Poor Elisha," were the first words out of Amber's mouth. Although she detested the girl, she could imagine how awful it would be to have your horses sold with no say in the matter. "To lose both of those lovely horses. So, what's that pony she's riding today?"

"It belongs to the Havershams. It's meant to be a good jumper, but it was bought for an eleven-year-old, and it's too much for them. Elisha's been asked to ride it and get it going again. I'm not sure if it's going to be for sale or if they're hoping to get the kid back on it. It bucked them off, and now they're terrified of it, apparently."

"Oh great. So now she'll be at everything we go to all summer?"

Chelsea shrugged. "Maybe. Don't know. But she's riding another one for someone else in the last two classes today as well. It looks like she's a rider for hire now, so she might be out and about quite a lot. Anyway, I'd better go and get Skye tacked up so I've got time to walk the course when this class finally ends. It's so busy!"

"Yeah, see you later."

No sooner had Chelsea disappeared than Emily was back by her side, Pink foaming at the mouth and lathered in white sweat. "I'm in the jump-off," Emily informed her before Amber had the chance to ask how she'd got on. "I need to go and wash her off before I go in again. Walk round with me?"

Pink didn't cooperate as Emily tried to sponge the sweat from the pony's face and body, spinning around in circles the whole time. "Will you stand STILL?" Emily bellowed at her. Pink just rolled her eyes and kept spinning. "Why is this pony such a psychopath?" she asked, looking over at their trailer in which Fudge was standing, quietly munching on his hay. "How did I go from him to you?"

Emily was full of the news about Elisha. "I wonder what's happened for him to lose everything and disappear?" she asked, lunging at Pink with the dripping sponge. "I wonder what'll happen to Troy now he can't hide behind Daddy's money?"

"Troy's Elisha's brother?" Amber asked. She hadn't known Elisha had a brother.

"Yeah, I'm surprised you've never heard of Troy Templeton. He's always in the paper for getting into trouble. He's done so much stuff, he should be in prison by now, but I'm sure Daddy has managed to keep him out by paying people off or whatever. He was expelled from school, and he's never had a job. Think he just expects to party through life using his parents' money to live on. He'll have to have a re-think now."

"Hmmm," Amber agreed. "So there'll be no more touring round the big shows with her horses and getting into *Horse & Hound* now then," she said, still thinking about Elisha, not her troublesome brother.

"Ha, no, there won't. She'll just have to ride whatever she can get her hands on now. There'll be no more looking down her nose at our 'second-rate' ponies and non-millionaire dads anymore. This is karma."

*Bit harsh,* Amber thought but then chastised herself for being too nice. After the way Elisha had treated both of them in the past, it was no wonder Emily was enjoying the idea of her being taken down a peg or two.

"Right, come on. I've got a jump-off to win," Emily declared, pulling herself back up into the saddle.

"Oh, really? Listen to you! Your dad will be delighted to hear that. What happened to Miss I'm-just-here-to-enjoy-myself-don't-care-about-winning Pryde?"

"That was before I knew *she* was here." Emily's face had that stern look about it again. The one she'd had earlier when she was annoyed with her dad for badgering Harry about having a pole down. "I've beaten her before, but that was only because she got eliminated. I want to beat her properly today. Come on, my pink pocket rocket. Let's go and show them how it's done."

# - Six -

## True Colours

Amber watched as the results were announced, and the top six riders rode into the arena to form a line. Despite its plunging and bucking in the first round, Elisha's mount had responded well to her urgent riding in the jump-off and had managed to be placed third. Emily had ridden like a demon and secured the fastest time, but a slight knock to the final plank fence, with the top plank resting on unforgiving flat cups had dropped her down to fourth place. As Emily took her place in the line-up beside Elisha to wait for the presentation of rosettes, Amber could see she was fuming.

*Don't say anything,* she willed her friend silently. *If you don't poke the snake, it won't bite.* But she could see

Elisha looking across at Pink, her trademark smirk tweaking the edge of her too-bright-to-be-real smile.

*Just look straight ahead. Don't engage with her. Ignore her.* Amber tried to catch Emily's eye in the hope she could convey her message through the expression on her face. But Emily wasn't looking in her direction. She was looking at Elisha.

"What?" Amber could just hear Emily's voice from where she sat astride Molly in the collecting ring. She was first to go in the next class,

*Oh no.* Amber groaned inwardly.

"Sorry?" Elisha asked, arranging her face into a look of sweet surprise.

"What are you smirking at?"

"I'm not. I was just admiring your pony. I haven't seen it before. It's very… different looking, isn't it, with that mane? Very punk rocker."

Emily didn't reply, uncertain whether Elisha was having a dig at Pink or merely stating a fact. Her hogged mane had grown out, but it was thick and coarse and stood up like a Mohican. If it were allowed to grow longer, it would flop over like a normal mane, but Emily liked her 'pink punk' and kept the mane as it was. There was no disputing that she was a unique-looking pony.

Amber saw Emily narrow her eyes and press her lips into a tight line, biting back any words she might have had ready, expecting to retaliate against some nasty comment.

"Such a shame you had that last fence down. You'd have won otherwise, with the fastest time."

Emily's lips pressed together so hard they disappeared completely, and even from a distance, Amber could see a red flush creeping up out of her collar, staining her ear lobes and her cheeks. She looked as if steam was going to come out of her ears from the effort it was taking her not to speak.

Elisha, again, was just stating a fact, but there was a tone in her voice that made the innocent words sound mocking. Anyone who didn't know her wouldn't have noticed, but Amber recognised it. The last time these two girls spoke to each other, Elisha had insulted Emily's beloved pony, Fudge, and her father, who was out of work at the time. It hadn't ended well, and Amber suspected that neither girl had forgiven the other. Both would love to get revenge, and at the moment, it was one-nil to Elisha.

"Better luck in the next class," Elisha said, smiling widely just as a member of the Highland Park staff pinned a yellow rosette to her pony's bridle.

"Thanks," Emily replied as the lady handed her a green rosette. Pink was curling her top lip up, showing her teeth in her trademark way, but it did look like she was getting ready to bite, and the lady gave her a wide berth. It wasn't clear if Emily's thanks were directed at Elisha or the rosette lady, but there was no mistaking where her next words were directed. "And how are things with you, Elisha? How's your dad?"

Elisha's eyes widened for the briefest of seconds, and a myriad emotions briefly betrayed her as they flickered across her face. But before she could respond, the lead rider was cantering away on the lap of honour, with the second-placed rider following, and she had to turn away. As the riders streamed out of the main arena, past Amber waiting at the entrance, she felt an unexpected pang of sympathy for Elisha.

"What did you say that to her for?" She frowned at Emily as her friend pulled Pink up beside her.

"Because she's being her usual snide self. Elisha might be trying to disguise it, but I know what she's up to. One of us has got to beat her in this round. Good luck!"

"Amber Anderson? Are you ready to go in?" the collecting ring steward asked, looking up from her clipboard. Amber nodded. "Then, in you go. They're just checking the height of the last couple of fences, so make sure you wait for the bell. Elisha Templeton – stand by."

Amber rode Molly into the arena at a walk, holding her breath as she waited for the bell to tell her to start. Looking around at the fences, she wished she could just ride straight back out again. *Why didn't I enter the 75cm and 85cm?* she asked herself as she rode past an oxer that now looked truly enormous. Molly hadn't warmed up well over the heightened practice fence and had even stopped at it twice. Amber couldn't understand how she could be so brilliant on a difficult 90cm cross-country course and then back off a show jumping course only a few centimetres higher.

Between worrying about Molly and being distracted by Emily's reaction to Elisha, Amber was again taken by surprise when the bell sounded to tell her to start her round. She was still just in walk, lost in thought.

“Oh, no! You idiot, you’ve done it again,” she chided herself, fussing Molly up into canter. “Come on girl, let’s do this.” Amber looked over her shoulder, searching for the first fence, ready to ride a good line at it this time. There it was. She looked at the top pole, but as she rode towards it, Caroline’s voice spoke in her head, ‘Don’t look *at* the jump Amber, look over it and beyond it. Look where you want to go!’

Amber raised her eyes to look beyond the pole and applied her legs to Molly’s sides. But as she did, when she looked at where she wanted to go, the sight that greeted her was Elisha Templeton, sitting astride her grey pony at the arena entrance, waiting to go next.

*Elisha is watching me!* Amber froze at the thought of Elisha watching her attempt a 95cm round for the first time. Instead of riding positively forward and infusing Molly with confidence and determination, she sat like a lump of coal. Molly jumped the fence awkwardly, and Amber heard the thud of a pole landing in the sand. *Great. Four faults at the first fence. That’s a brilliant start. Get a grip!*

Amber needed to ride how she’d ridden in the recent tetrathlon. She tried to summon the feeling she’d had when Keira Marshall-Digby had attempted to discourage her by admitting to stealing Chelsea's bridle. She'd been so full of outrage, it had fuelled her to ride with a determination that saw them get a clear round on a difficult, technical track. Amber needed that now. She needed to show Elisha that she could do the bigger classes. She'd progressed. Amber was in the same league as other riders her age.

But it wasn't there. There was no fire in her today, and Amber couldn't summon any. Knowing that Elisha's eyes were on her extinguished all her confidence…and her riding ability, it seemed.

They got over the second and third fences, but fence four: the oxer, which was right next to the arena entrance where Elisha sat, was the end. On the first presentation at the fence, Molly failed to take off, sliding into the fillers and sending poles flying. A buzzer sounded, and a crew of course stewards ran in to reassemble it while Amber prepared to re-present.

"Come on, Mols," she pleaded, "please jump it. I can't get eliminated right under *her* nose."

But, when the fence was re-built, and Amber rode strongly at it, Molly pulled herself up in front of it again and threw her head back as if she didn't want to even look at it.

"I'm sorry, but that's elimination," said a voice on the loudspeaker, telling her what she already knew.

Amber rode towards the exit, keeping her head down. She didn't want anyone to see the tears welling in her eyes, and especially not Elisha. *Hopefully she'll have come straight in, and I won't have to pass her,* she thought.

But no. Instead of cantering in, ready to start, Elisha rode past Amber at a walk. As they passed, Elisha leaned over towards her.

"It's criminal what you've done to that pony," she said. "You've ruined her. If Frankie Drake could see Molly now, she wouldn't recognise her."

Elisha booted her pony and cantered away. Amber's ears burned as the tears she held inside fought for release.

Emily rode towards her, and the look of pity and concern on her face was too much. She should have been the rider to follow Amber. They'd entered at the same time and should have been one after another. But because Elisha was riding some other horse in this class, they'd put her inbetween them to give her time to warm her second ride up. If Emily had been there watching, willing her on, would it have gone differently? Would she still have been eliminated?

A huge sob broke free, releasing tears that spilled over her cheeks and blurred her vision.

"Amber?" She heard Emily's voice, but she rode straight past. She didn't want to speak to anyone.

Molly was untacked, rugged, booted and loaded into the trailer in silence. Her parents seemed to understand that this wasn't the time for questions and explanations, and she made sure that she didn't have to say anything all the way home. Amber rammed her headphones in and listened to loud music, trying to drown out the voices clamouring to make themselves heard in her head.

*Fancy just leaving like that. You didn't stay to watch Emily or Chelsea's rounds. What will they think? Some friend.*

*There you were thinking you were going to have Georgia looking up to you and being inspired by you! Ha ha! Pur-lease. Who'd be inspired by you? You're useless.*

*SHUT UP!* She closed her eyes and tried to focus on the song's upbeat lyrics; some pop princess rattling on about loving yourself and how everyone's perfect. But the message of positivity was drowned out as Elisha's venomous words set up a cycle in her mind, going round and round in a loop, with more joining in to torment her.

*You've ruined that pony. She was good before you got her, but now, she's unrecognisable. It's all your fault. Poor Molly.*

# - Seven -

## Moving On

"You haven't ruined her at all," Mrs Anderson said, stroking Amber's hair that night. She'd just popped in to say goodnight seeing that Amber's bedroom light was still on, and found her sobbing silently into her pillow. Stig, the cat – that wasn't allowed in the bedroom – purred loudly as she ran her hand over him.

Amber began to protest, but her mother shushed her. "Yes, you've had some falls and failures with her, but they're not failures when you get back up and keep trying, which you have." She wedged herself into the sliver of space beside her daughter on the bed and continued stroking her hair soothingly. This was how she'd got Amber to go to sleep when she was young, but that was a long time ago. She noticed how even Amber's hair felt more grown-up now. It no longer had the fine, silky texture of a child's. The strands were thick and wiry, much like her own.

"Honestly, Amber, Dad and I are so proud of what you've achieved with Molly. You've faced fear so many times. You've had the opportunity to give up with her, but you haven't. The way you've blamed yourself for everything and looked for ways to improve yourself and your riding shows discipline and responsibility, but it's not all your fault. Give yourself a break." She paused, still stroking her daughter's hair, thinking how to go on to what she wanted to say next. Amber didn't speak, and the sobs had faded to the occasional hiccough. Mrs Anderson took a deep breath and continued.

"We want to see you have fun again," she began. "And it would be nice to see Molly have some fun too."

Amber turned her face up towards her mother, wondering what she was meaning.

"Molly's seventeen now. I know many ponies go on longer than that, but I think she needs to retire from being a Pony Club pony, pet. I know she's enjoyed the cross-country recently, but there aren't many cross-country competitions compared to show jumping. When we unload Molly, and she's sees its show jumping, she looks bored. In fact, I think she looks sad." Mrs Anderson looked down into Amber's red-rimmed eyes.

"I've spoken to a few people who've known her in the past, and she's done this all her life, Amber. I don't think she wants to do it anymore. Dad and I think we should look for a non-competitive home for her and get you another pony, or perhaps even a little horse…"

A soft flutter of joy rippled through her at the thought of a new horse. She imagined having a horse that loved to jump and finally being able to hold her own against Elisha. The thought of not having to struggle with Molly anymore was such a relief. Noticing how she immediately felt lighter, happier, more relaxed at the mere mention of moving on from the pony, Amber hadn't realised how weighed down she'd been before. Her mum was right. It was time to call it a day with Molly.

But although she knew this was the right decision, it didn't stop her heart from turning into a boulder at the thought of actually giving up on Molly and letting her go to someone else. The pony was a living being, not just an object without feelings. The boulder inside her grew so heavy, it felt real.

"But…" she began.

"I know what you're going to say," Mrs Anderson interrupted her, "but we're not going to sell her to just anyone. We'll make sure it's a good home. In fact, there's a woman who comes into my shop. She's often wearing riding clothes, so I got chatting with her. Turns out she's had a pony on loan for a couple of years, but it's going back to its owners soon so she's on the lookout for one to buy for herself. She's only small, smaller than you, and she just does hacking and a bit of endurance, but she doesn't want a plod. She likes a lively ride. Molly could be perfect for her."

Amber turned around to face her mother and pushed herself up into a sitting position, taking care not to squash the cat. "Do you mean, like now? Straight away? But it's the summer holidays. I'll have nothing to ride or take to shows. I can't take Pearl," she said, picturing Elisha's face if she saw Amber back on the Fell pony. She could just imagine how Elisha would revel in telling everyone that Awful Amber had caused a previously successful competition pony to have to retire.

"Well, this woman might not buy Molly. She'll have to come and try her and see if she likes her. But either way, I don't think Molly should go to any more shows. It isn't doing either of you any good. And, we were talking to Chelsea's mum today. She knows someone with a little horse they want to loan out. I don't think it's done much, but Victoria thinks it's a nice type and that you could have some fun bringing it on. We could go and see it?"

Amber thought about how freeing it would be to bring on a horse that no-one knew and had no expectations of. She could legitimately take it in the smaller classes without anybody questioning it, and there would be no pressure. Elisha wouldn't be going near the small classes, so it would mean she could stay out of her way if she would be popping up everywhere all summer.

Amber nodded. Decision made.

"Okay, well, in the morning, I'll give Victoria a ring and get the number. Now," she leaned over Amber and scooped up the black and white cat, "get some sleep and stop worrying."

***

The visit to see the horse-for-loan was quickly arranged for tea time the following day. After checking on their own ponies in the morning, Amber had a relaxing day reading in the garden. Or at least she read when she wasn't on her phone, messaging Emily, Chelsea and JoJo. She told them her news and was surprised that they were all full of encouragement. She'd expected some shock and outrage that she was selling Molly and going to look at another horse while Molly grazed, oblivious in the field, and had considered not telling them. But they were her friends. She hadn't told them when she chose to ride Honey in the branch tetrathlon for fear of what they would say, but when they found out, none of them were bothered. She trusted them.

It's like I've told you before, Emily typed. Some horses and riders just aren't suited. Don't feel bad. It's just how it is. Molly might be happier with someone else and you too, with a different horse.

This is my last season on Skye, Chelsea replied. I'm doing a few more BE100's to give her more of a record, then I'll be selling her to get a young event horse. She's a great pony, but I'm fifteen soon and growing out of her. I need to move onto horses.

As well as their views on her plans, Amber also found out what had happened at the show after she left. Chelsea had won the 95cm, and the 105cm class on Skye, thanks to her previous life as a show jumper, and Emily had managed to come second on Pink, in the 95cm, which she was delighted about. Elisha's grey pony hadn't made it into the jump-off after it decided to nap back to the collecting ring and got itself eliminated at the same fence that claimed Amber.

She shouldn't have sat there for so long watching you! I took great delight in saying 'what a shame,' as I passed her on my way in. She looked absolutely furious 😠

But Elisha's second ride had gone much better. It was a horse whose rider had been away at university and was now on holiday with her step-family. Elisha had been asked to take it out and get it going again, ready for its rider to take over when she got back. It jumped double clear in both rounds, coming fourth in the 95cm and second in the 105cm. At least it sounded like she wouldn't have the ride on it for long if its owner was coming back, but the grey definitely needed an experienced hand for a while longer if it was going to be suitable for an eleven-year-old. Elisha would be at every show they went to this summer.

***

At 5pm, the wait was over, and the Andersons got in the car to go and view the loan horse. They headed in the direction of Gosforth, but soon they branched off down narrow, twisty country lanes, leaving Amber with no idea where they were going.

The hedgerow-lined roads seemed to go on forever, with just a couple of houses tucked in so tightly, it was like they were hiding. Only their gates, set into the hedgerow, gave them away. Eventually, they climbed up an even narrower lane and onto the driveway of a pretty bungalow. The gardens were a mass of mature trees and shrubs with a lawn that looked like a bowling green.

Before they'd even got out of the car, an immaculately dressed woman stepped out of the front door. She didn't look like someone about to go into a stable and tack up a horse. She was wearing khaki chinos, and a crisp white shirt with a mustard-coloured scarf arranged loosely around her shoulders. Her fingernails were long and red, her dark shoulder-length hair perfectly styled. Sunglasses covered most of her face, but her lips matched her nails. *Crikey,* thought Amber, who was wearing her everyday riding gear, *who is she?*

She turned out to be Anita. Lover of Shetland ponies. They were everywhere. As she took them round the back, they passed paddocks full of Shetland ponies in every colour. She bred them, apparently. There was a pristine outdoor menage with glossy poles lining the edges and show jump wings stacked in the corners. The stables were inside a barn. Everything was as neat as a pin, like a professional yard.

Anita pushed her sunglasses up onto her head when they entered the barn, revealing a face that was older than Amber had first thought. Amber guessed her age to be around sixty. "And here he is," she indicated one of the stables with a long, red nail. "This is Darcy."

Amber looked at the face hanging over the stable door, just as a girl a bit older than her appeared out of nowhere and slipped a head collar over the face. She opened the door and led the horse out.

He was beautiful. Plain – without a single white hair anywhere on him, but clearly a fine, well-bred animal. He was the colour of caramel with black legs and silky black mane and tail. He wasn't much more than a pony at around 15hh, with a small, delicate head and slender neck.

The girl didn't receive any instructions from Anita, so must have been briefed in advance as a saddle and bridle were quickly produced, and Darcy was ready to ride.

"I bought him for showing," Anita informed them as the girl, yet to be introduced, led the horse towards the arena, "but he has an annoying habit of nodding his head, so he's no good as a show horse. Too excitable. If he was a mare, I'd put him in foal, but he's not and I haven't got a job for him. I don't really want to sell him as he's such a handsome little thing, but it'd be nice to see him out and about doing something. Megan here rides him sometimes when she's got time," she waved her hand in the girl's direction, "but he's done very little."

"How old is he?" Mrs Anderson asked.

"He's… eight? Yes, eight. So it's time he started doing more than being a field ornament."

They arrived at the manege, and Anita opened the gate for Megan, who quickly mounted and gave them a quick show of Darcy's paces. For a horse who'd had very little time spent on him, he looked well-schooled to Amber.

"Has he done any jumping?" Mr Anderson asked.

"Oh no, Megan doesn't jump, and I certainly don't," she chuckled. "The jumps are there for the livery clients' use. But you're welcome to try him."

Amber felt her familiar nerves as she switched places with Megan and began riding with everyone watching. But she soon relaxed. He felt glorious. Amber imagined this was what it felt like to ride a professional sports horse like the ones she saw on the TV. Darcy was as supple as a piece of plasticine. And so responsive! She only had to give the lightest of aids, and he reacted instantly. It was like magic. She couldn't wait to try him over a jump.

Mr Anderson dragged some poles out to start with, which Darcy happily trotted and cantered over, then he set up a couple of small jumps. While he was fiddling with cups and poles, Amber let Darcy stand and have a rest.

"There, look, he's doing it!" Anita cried.

"What?" Amber looked down, wondering what the horse was doing. It was nothing she could see or feel.

"The head nodding! It's what he does when he's excited."

Amber nearly laughed. If this was all the little horse did when he was excited, she'd have nothing to worry about. He remained stock-still, but now that it had been pointed out, she could see that he was making a slight nodding motion. He looked like someone listening to music, gently nodding along to the beat. It was such a tiny movement; she hadn't noticed it. If this was the 'excitability' that had ruined his future career as a show horse, she imagined that show horses must be very dull indeed.

When presented with his first small jumps, Darcy hopped over them as if he knew exactly what was expected of him. As the horse was enthusiastic but calm, the fences were raised a couple of times until they were popping over 80cm effortlessly.

"Happy?" Mrs Anderson asked Amber as she patted and dismounted Darcy.

Amber nodded, smiling widely.

"Thought so."

"He's amazing. They say he hasn't done a lot, but he seems to know what he's doing. He'll be great in no time." Amber ran her stirrups up and slackened the girth, giving Darcy a loving rub between the eyes.

"So, we'll say we'll have him then?"

Amber nodded, but her smile faded. This would mean the end for her and Molly, after all they'd been through and the work she'd put in. But riding Darcy showed her that Molly wasn't the right pony for her. When she rode Molly, there was always a niggle of uncertainty about what she might do. Amber realised that she was never one hundred per cent relaxed on Molly. She'd only ridden Darcy for a short time, but she'd felt that 'click' with him. It was as if they knew each other well, rather than having just met. She'd felt safe and relaxed and happy with him. Wasn't that what riding was meant to be about? How often could she truly say she'd felt like that when riding Molly?

"I think we'd be happier taking him if you'd tried him on a hack too, love. Why don't you get back on and go for a little ride out on him while we have a chat with Anita and see what's what?"

***

Darcy was just as lovely out on a ride as he was in the arena, and when Amber arrived back at the yard, she was more certain than ever that he was the horse for her.

"So, we've discussed it with Anita and said we'll have him, but that we need to sell Molly before he can come to us as we haven't a stable to put him in at the moment." Mrs Anderson spoke to Amber over her shoulder as they drove out of Anita's gates. "Okay?"

"Uh-huh," Amber agreed, not wanting to think about saying goodbye to Molly.

"I'll get in touch with that woman I told you about then, and see if she'd like to come and try her. Fingers crossed she likes her.

"Yeah, fingers crossed." Amber looked down at her hands. Slowly she crossed her right middle finger over the index finger and stared at them until her vision blurred.

# - Eight -

# Goodbye

Mrs Anderson had been right. Her 'shop lady', who turned out to be called Celia, had been on the lookout for a new pony, and Molly had proved to be just what she was looking for. Celia had been to the yard a couple of times to try Molly, and she'd also wanted to catch her and bring her in from the field, groom her, tack her up and try her ridden in company and on her own.

When Celia had told Mrs Anderson she would like to buy Molly, Amber hadn't been as upset as she'd expected to be. Partly because Celia was so nice, and partly because she hadn't rushed into buying Molly like they had. Celia visited twice and spent a lot of time with the pony. She'd groomed her thoroughly, taken time to check her tack over to assess that everything was a good fit, and Amber liked that she constantly talked to the pony and patted her often.

So when Celia rattled into the farmyard with her trailer to collect Molly, Amber kept her composure. While Celia chatted to her parents in the yard, Amber gave Molly a last hug and kissed her muzzle. She didn't linger over it as she knew that to do so would bring tears, so she clipped Molly's lead rope to her head collar and led her out of the stable, handing her to her new owner.

"And it's goodbye to Molly," said Georgia, who had just arrived with her dad, for a ride on Pearl. She stood beside Amber and watched Celia load Molly. Georgia had known this was happening today, as Mr Anderson had told her dad. Although she'd only met Molly a couple of times, Georgia wanted to be there to see her off.

She left Amber's side and stood beside the trailer's jockey door, peering inside at Molly, who was tugging at a haynet.

"Goodbye, girl," Georgia said, reaching in to offer Molly her leaving present. She opened her fist and held out her palm to reveal three sugar lumps. Molly blew gently on them before curling her lips around the offering and crunching them up.

"I brought you something too." Georgia came back to Amber and held out a brown paper bag containing some milk chocolate chip cookies. "So you wouldn't feel too sad. Chocolate makes everything better."

Amber took the cookies and smiled, thinking that Emily would agree with that sentiment. "Thanks, Georgia." She'd wanted to add, *that's really kind of you,* but her throat chose that moment to close up and seal the words inside. She swallowed them back down before she choked.

"I'll take good care of her, Amber." Celia appeared and pulled her into a hug. "I'll be forever posting pictures of her online, so you'll always be able to see what we're up to. And if you ever want to come and visit her, just let me know; you're always welcome."

"Uh-huh," Amber replied, her words still held back by the tears that burned her throat.

"And thanks so much for including her tack in the sale," Celia turned to Amber's parents. "That saddle is so comfortable and such a good fit on her. It's a huge relief to know I don't have to start saddle shopping when I get her home."

"It's a pleasure," Mrs Anderson said. "We're happy to let it go with her as, like you say, it's such a good fit. Enjoy her."

"Oh, I will!" Celia said, hugging Mrs Anderson, followed by a rather startled Mr Anderson. "We're going to have the *best* time. I can't wait for everyone on the yard to see my new pony!" She sounded like an excited little girl, not a forty-something-year-old woman.

Celia checked the trailer and climbed into her car, driving off in a crunch of gravel. They all stood for a minute and listened to the trailer bumping its way down the farm track until it was out of earshot. Amber released a breath she hadn't known she'd been holding.

"That's that then," she said.

"It is. I know it's sad, but she's going to a lovely person, and it means I can ring Anita and arrange to bring Darcy here," Mrs Anderson said, looking across at their pony trailer. "I know Darcy isn't much bigger than Molly, but do you think he'll fit in our wee trailer?" she asked her husband. They both walked in the trailer's direction to inspect it.

To keep her mind off the vision of Molly being taken to a new and unfamiliar place, Amber briskly turned away and headed back to the Fell ponies to get Pearl ready for her lesson.

Georgia had ridden Pearl twice since returning from her holiday, and Amber had noticed a decrease in the number of *my instructor says* in response to the advice Amber gave her. According to Georgia's dad, there was now a lot of *Amber says* in their house: not just from Georgia, but from her two younger brothers who kept mimicking *Amber says* whenever their sister mentioned ponies.

Amber didn't know whether it was because she'd decided to be more patient with the younger girl or because Georgia was making a special effort not to be annoying, but she found her much more tolerable now than when they'd first met.

With Molly gone and Honey not quite fit for riding due to her sore eye, Georgia's ride was a lesson in the small paddock. Unfortunately, Pearl wasn't in the mood, preferring to spend her time stopping and snatching for grass.

"Ahhh, no. Stop that!" Georgia yanked the reins and gave Pearl a big kick in an attempt to get the naughty pony moving.

Amber sighed, resolving to channel Caroline's quiet, patient manner. She knew how stubborn Pearl could be. It wasn't Georgia's fault; the pony was testing her new rider to see what she could get away with. Amber remembered how JoJo had encouraged her when she was just starting out and how Elisha had sneered. She remembered too, how the girl's smug superiority had threatened to ruin her relationship with Pearl. It was up to her to pass on everything she'd learned to Georgia and build her confidence like her friends and Caroline had done for her.

"Don't worry, it's not you. Pearl can be a pain sometimes, and she'll try anything to get out of having to work." Amber approached the headless pony – whose whole face had disappeared into a clump of long grass – and pulled her away from it.

"Come on, you little wotsit." She walked Pearl away from the edge of the paddock before letting Georgia take back the reins. "Time to work!" She gave Pearl a little slap on the bottom to wake her up.

"Thanks," Georgia said gratefully.

***

The lesson went well. Georgia was actually a pretty good rider. She wasn't rough, but she wasn't a wet lettuce either, who just sat there waiting to be told everything. Just as Amber noticed Pearl was about to slow down for a grass-snatch, and prepared to warn Georgia to ride her on, the girl felt Pearl's change of pace herself and pushed her on. She trotted in good balance and didn't hang on to the reins to support herself anymore. Amber was impressed. But when Georgia started eyeing up the barrel jump and asked if she could have a go, the memory of Pearl dumping Mrs Anderson into the nettle patch beside it rang in her head like a warning siren.

"Er, maybe not yet. We'll leave jumping for another day. But you've done really well today."

Georgia was clearly delighted with the compliment and chattered non-stop all the way back to the stable. Amber couldn't have said what she'd talked about, as she wasn't listening. She was just enjoying the way Georgia's happiness took her mind off Molly as they passed her empty stable.

"You know," Mrs Anderson said as they drove home, dropping Georgia off on their way, "now you're getting Darcy, and Honey will be back in work soon, you're not going to have much time for Pearl, and Georgia loves her. Why don't we see if she'd like to have Pearl on loan? Staying at the farm, of course."

Amber instinctively bristled at the thought of someone else having her Pearl, but it was true. With all her attention going to Molly recently, Pearl had been side lined. And now she was getting her first horse, that was unlikely to change. It would be nice for Pearl to be someone's priority again. Imagining Georgia's reaction to finding out Pearl was hers made Amber smile. And she'd still see her pony every day if she was staying at the farm. Pearl would still be Honey's best friend. It seemed like a perfect idea.

"Yeah, I think Georgia'd love that," she said.

"And what about you? Are you happy with it?"

"Like you say, I'll be busy with Darcy so it would be nice for Pearl to have someone who's focussed on her."

Mrs Anderson laughed. "Oh, I'm sure Pearl will love to have someone coming to ride her every day instead of getting nice days off stuffing her face in the field!"

Amber chuckled. "Well, it'll be good for her waistline, at least!"

"That's true. I'll give Mr Lockwood a ring after tea and suggest it. And I'll try Anita again too. I've been trying to contact her, but I haven't been able to get hold of her."

Amber twitched with excitement. There was still a morsel of worry about how Molly would be doing in her new home, but the thought of Darcy arriving made her somehow feel lighter and freer. It was like being released from the relationship with Molly had taken a weight from her shoulders. It was a strange mix of guilt and hope that took turns unsettling her then cheering her.

She tried to put Molly out of her mind and think about the future. Not everything with Molly had been a failure, and the pony had definitely brought her on massively as a rider. She'd be happy in her new home, and Amber would be happy with Darcy.

The rest of the summer holidays was going to be amazing.

# - Nine -

## Change of Heart

"Do you want the good news or the bad?" Mrs Anderson said.

If Amber had been paying more attention, she'd have realised that the bad news must be bad as her mother made no mention of Stig curled up beside Amber on the bed. But she'd been distracted, messaging her friends on her phone. Chelsea was telling them that her competition with Skye this coming weekend might be her last, as the pony would be advertised for sale at the event. Chelsea was at the top of the young rider points league in the Cumbrian events, and she was being noticed. Skye was sure to be snapped up. Although they were only communicating through messages, Amber could tell that Chelsea was conflicted. She was ambitious and wanted to get a young horse to move up through the eventing levels with, but she was attached to Skye. She'd worked hard to move the pony from show jumping to eventing, and Skye had rewarded her with several top placings during the season so far. It would be hard to part with the pony who'd helped her get there.

Amber was lost in her words. Chelsea was getting a horse. But then, so was she. And in fact, she was the first one of her friends to do so. It was the beginning of the end of an era as they all started moving off their beloved ponies. And she was the one leading the way. It was an unfamiliar feeling.

Amber looked up from her phone but didn't get a chance to reply as Mrs Anderson bowled on.

"The good news is that Georgia is over the moon about having Pearl on loan. I asked her dad, and he rang me back within five minutes to say yes. So, she's delighted. That's nice, isn't it?"

"Yeah, it's great." Amber eyed her mother with suspicion. Her voice was a higher pitch than usual, as if she was trying to make herself seem enthusiastic, and she seemed strangely animated. "What's the bad news?"

Mrs Anderson interlocked her fingers and squeezed so tightly her knuckles turned white. "Well, I finally got hold of Anita to let her know that we've got space for Darcy now so we could come and collect him, and...she...er...she said she'd changed her mind."

"Changed...her... mind?" Amber echoed slowly, as if she didn't understand the words.

"Apparently. Anita said she's thought about it and decided that she doesn't want some child rider charging about on him, spoiling him..."

"I'm not a *child.* And I wouldn't be *charging about on him!*"

"I said that to her. I told her you aren't that kind of rider – that you're having lessons with someone who's very gentle in the way they ride and teach, but she wasn't having it. She was quite rude, actually, and I'm annoyed by her attitude. I told her that your pony has gone and you've nothing to ride now, but she wasn't interested."

Amber flung her phone down on the bed with such force, it bounced off and landed on the carpet. Stig woke, alarmed by the sudden movement, and leapt off the bed too, pushing past Mrs Anderson's legs in the doorway.

"There's four weeks left of the summer holidays, and I've got nothing to ride! I'm going to miss *everything*."

"I'll speak to the vet and see if Honey can start being ridden soon, but, yes, this has mucked everything up. Darcy seemed perfect for you. We'll have to start looking for something else. And I think we'll be looking for horses for sale, not for loan. We don't want this to happen again."

Amber stared back at her but didn't speak. Mrs Anderson fidgeted in the doorway, unsure what else she could say or do. When Amber still didn't speak, her mother turned and padded away down the stairs. With the door still open, Amber could hear her parents' muffled voices. She could guess what they'd be saying.

Leaning over the bed, she bent down and scooped up her phone. Returning to the group message, she told JoJo, Chelsea and Emily all about it.

***

"That's terrible news," Caroline said as she pulled Lady up and gave her a pat.

They'd picked Georgia up on their way to the yard, and her excitement about Pearl was annoying Amber. It was like salt being rubbed in the wound as she brooded about Darcy. When they pulled up in the yard, and Amber had spotted Caroline riding in the small paddock, she'd excused herself to go and watch, leaving her mum and Georgia to go and get the Fell ponies in from the field.

"This all looks…interesting," Amber changed the subject, indicating the range of obstacles Caroline had set up in the paddock. There was a pair of blue barrels standing on their ends, a pair of wheelie bins pushed together and a ratty old arm chair that usually lived in the hay barn. All of them had broom handles leaning against them. Amber guessed they were meant to act as the flags on cross-country fences.

Caroline slid down from Lady's back and ran her stirrups up, laughing but blushing at the same time. She was much more confident speaking to Amber and her parents these days, but she was still shy. It was part of what made Amber love her so much; her complete lack of ego or arrogance.

"We're doing our first BE100 on Sunday, and I just wanted to give her some practice at some higher skinnies. She's seen a corner and an arrowhead doing the 90s, but a 100 course is likely to be a bit more technical.

I've just had to use whatever I could find. But if Lady will jump these okay, she should be fine with whatever we come across on a professionally built cross-country course. There'll be no wheelie bins or armchairs there!"

Amber laughed, grateful to Caroline for taking her mind off the disappointment gnawing its way through her.

"My friend Chelsea is doing a BE100 on Sunday too. She says it's a new event at Brotherby. Is that where you're going?"

"It is." Caroline started leading Lady out of the paddock and across the farm yard. Amber followed. "I'm not quite sure where it is, and I don't have anybody coming with me this weekend, so I'll have to set off pretty early to make sure I find it in time."

Amber's ears pricked up. "You don't have anyone going to help you? I could come and be your groom! I've never been to a BE event before."

They reached the stable, and Caroline brought Lady inside, pulling the stable door closed. Amber opened it and followed them inside, removing Lady's bridle while Caroline unbuckled the girth, proving how helpful she could be.

"That would be great Amber, but I'm doing dressage at 8.30am, so I'll be leaving here *really* early in the morning. You could always come to the event with your parents to watch. Then you won't have to get up at the crack of dawn."

"No, I want to come with you and be your groom, to help! I don't mind getting up early. And I'm sure my dad is on first shift at the weekend, so he'll be coming in this direction at about half five in the morning. He could drop me off in the layby in the dual carriageway, and you could pick me up there?"

"I think I'd better have a chat with your mum about it," Caroline said, just as Mrs Anderson passed her stable, leading Honey. "But, yeah, it'd be great to have a travelling groom with me!"

On Sunday morning, Amber had no trouble getting out of bed at 5am. Normally she wasn't a morning person and hated getting up for school, but this was different. Amber had only ever seen Caroline riding on the farm lane and in the paddock, but today she'd be watching her take on other riders. It would be the first time she'd see Lady competing too. Lady-the-dangerous-racehorse-who-nobody-would-touch-with-a-bargepole taking on horses that had been trained specifically for the sport of eventing. There might even be some famous riders from the telly competing their young horses. It was so exciting, she might as well have been going to Badminton.

Mr Anderson had phoned into work to say that he might be a little late getting in as he had to drop his daughter off and didn't want to leave her standing in a layby at 6 o clock in the morning by herself. He needn't have worried as Caroline's lorry pulled in at 5.55am. Amber scrambled out of the car, dragging her stuff with her and ignoring her dad's questions of 'have you got your phone? Have you got your waterproof, just in case? Have you got your purse?' She gave him a distracted wave before hauling open the passenger door of the lorry and pulling herself up into the cab.

"Morning!" she cried, brightly.

"Wow, you're wide awake for this time of day," Caroline gave Mr Anderson a wave and a thumbs-up before pulling back out onto the road and continuing their journey, "which is good because you're the navigator. I've been told that trying to use satnav to find it is no good, so are you okay to use Google Maps to direct me?" Amber saw a piece of paper with an address written on it lying on the spare passenger seat and picked it up.

"Right. First mission of the day: get us to the right place." Amber pulled her phone out of her pocket and typed the address in, bringing it closer to her face. She'd forgotten to bring her glasses amongst the pile of kit she'd come armed with, thinking she wouldn't need them. She was determined to impress Caroline and make sure they got to where they needed to be in time. Amber had planned to use the travelling time to interview Caroline and find out more about her. It struck her that she didn't really know anything about the young woman she so admired, and this would be her chance to find out. But she couldn't do that and concentrate on keeping up with the directions at the same time. It would have to wait until the return journey.

By the time they pulled into the event and were pointed in the direction of the lorry parking area, Amber felt sick from snaking along narrow country roads. She might as well have been on a fairground waltzer ride for the last 90 minutes. When the lorry finally pulled up, and

Amber opened the cab door, she almost fell out onto the damp grass.

"You okay? You look as green as that grass," Caroline observed with concern as she climbed down. "Just get some fresh air and have a rest while I go and get my number and pay the start fee."

Amber made an 'okay' sign with her fingers as she leant back against the lorry, breathing deeply. The smells were comforting. Even at this early hour, she could smell fly spray, hay, damp mud and horse manure.

As Caroline made her way towards the white tents in the distance, Amber observed the bustle of the competitors and their helpers. Some horses were tied to lorries so huge and grand, they looked more expensive than Amber's house. And the horses themselves were the picture of perfection: exactly what you'd expect event horses to look like, with their fit, muscular bodies, tiny plaits, pulled tails and glossy coats. Here she was, leaning against the Blakely's cattle wagon, knowing that the horse it held inside did not match up to these beauties. Nerves swelled inside her, even though she wasn't the one riding today. Could Lady go up against these horses? She was fit, but she was lean and lacked muscle. And whereas most thoroughbreds had neat little ears and thin, silky manes and tails, Caroline joked that Lady was a 'thoroughbred mule' due to her large, floppy ears. To top it off, the horse had the bushiest mane Amber had ever seen on a non-native. When she'd first arrived, Lady's mane had a centre parting and fell equally on both sides of her neck. Caroline had tried to tidy it up by pulling it and training it to lie on one side only, but now it just wanted to stick up in the air like Pink's Mohican mane. Amber guessed that she would not have a neck full of tiny, neat plaits when she came out of the lorry. They'd probably resemble the golf balls that Emily's pony, Fudge, sported whenever his thick mane was forced into plaits.

*But it doesn't matter what they look like,* Amber thought as the fresh morning air invigorated her. *It's not showing. This is about finding out which horses have it all: obedience, bravery and accuracy. If Caroline has entered her, then she must have faith in her. And so do I, because with Caroline riding her, she already has a head start on every horse here.*

"Right, my lady," Amber called as she lowered the ramp of the lorry. "Let's get you out and ready for some action.” The riding might be up to Caroline today, but Amber was going to do everything she could to help. That way Caroline would have nothing to worry about and could concentrate on what she needed to: remembering times, remembering tests and courses, and of course, riding.

Amber tied Lady to the lorry and nodded. She was right about those plaits. “First job, Miss, is to get you looking your best. And I think we’ll start with tidying up those plaits!”

When Caroline returned to the lorry with her number tucked under her arm, her head was down, and her lips were moving. Amber recognised the look of pained concentration on her face – she was running through her dressage test, speaking the movements in a whisper as she ran through them in her mind. But despite the intensity of her focus on the test, as soon as she saw Lady, she noticed.

"Oh, wow, Amber, she looks so much better now. You're obviously much better at plaiting than me. Thank you! And you've got her all tacked up for me too." She looked Amber right in the eye for once. "You're amazing."

"No problem." It was Amber's turn to look down, Caroline's compliment suddenly making her shy. "I'll take her for a walk around to loosen up while you get changed." Amber removed Lady's head collar and took hold of her reins, leading her away from the lorry. The mare quietly followed, her hot breath blowing on the back of Amber's hand.

"So, you, I hope you're going to be a lady today," she spoke quietly into the mare's plain face beside her as she observed some of the competitors warming up for their tests, looking like Olympians. "You don't have to win today, just be good and look after Caroline. I know it probably wasn't your fault what happened to your last rider, but Caroline has put a lot of faith into you, so well, yeah. Just look after her, okay? That's all."

This would've been the point where Pearl would nudge her in the chest, but Lady just regarded her quietly with soft brown eyes. Tears pricked in Amber's eyes as a sudden wave of emotion came out of nowhere. She blinked them away rapidly as Caroline approached them, now looking nearly perfect in her dressage outfit. A few strands of wavy brown hair that had escaped the hairnet caught Amber's attention and reminded her that this pair weren't some elite professional partnership; they were just Caroline and Lady from the farm.

"Good luck," Amber said as Caroline mounted and rode towards the warm-up area. She hoped they wouldn't need it.

***

"I can't believe you were in the top ten in your first BE100!" Amber stroked the large, blue rosette displaying a gold number eight in the centre, yet again as they drove towards home later that day. It meant as much to her as if she'd won it herself.

"I know," Caroline said, keeping her eyes on the road. "I wasn't expecting that. She's getting better in the dressage – her balance is improving, and she's accepting a contact more. She feels less like riding an ironing board now, but she's still got a way to go to get into the scores that normally get placed."

"Yeah, but her jumping was fab. That's what moved her up the scoreboard so much." Amber was so excited, she didn't even care that she was telling Caroline something she already knew. "When my friend Chelsea saw you jumping, she didn't believe me when I said Lady has been a racer until recently. She said her shape over a fence was perfect." Amber had bumped into Chelsea, who was riding Skylark in a different section. When she'd pointed Lady out to her, Chelsea had praised the mare no end, noticing how straight to a fence and how careful over it she was.

"Going clear in the show jumping was more than I hoped for, watching the ones in before me. The double and the upright after it were causing some trouble today, but she was so easy to ride. She listened and waited and just jumped out of her skin. She was so careful and really tried not to touch a pole."

"Yeah, she was amazing. And then there was the cross-country," Amber was enjoying reliving the day now that all her nerves about Lady's behaviour had passed. "She didn't hesitate at anything. Even the brush fence they'd made to look like a hedgehog. There were a few who ducked out at that one."

"Mm-hm, I think the practising over wheelie bins and armchairs must have paid off!"

They both laughed, then Amber slumped back in her chair, gazing at the huge rosette again, stroking its silky folds and pleats. It was only a rosette, but it represented a huge achievement. The lorry rolled along while its driver and passenger descended into silence, and their own thoughts.

*How can it be*, wondered Amber, *that Caroline is so shy and worried about some things, yet she can take on a horse with Lady's reputation and, in no time, have her competing successfully at that level? She's brilliant, so why isn't she more confident? What could I say to ask her that doesn't sound nosey?*

"You've gone quiet," Caroline said, helpfully breaking the silence, and glancing over at Amber.

"Yeah, er…I was just thinking, well wondering really. You're a *really* good rider, and a brilliant teacher... So, you know, I'd have thought you'd be a bit more…?" she searched for a word that wouldn't make her sound cheeky.

"Confident?" Caroline provided.

"Well, er… yeah. Sorry, I don't mean to sound rude, but if I was like you, as good as you, I mean, I'd, er…" Amber struggled to find the words she was trying to say and trailed off.

"Confidence is a funny thing," Caroline replied quietly, keeping her eyes forward. "It can take years to build up, but it can be lost in a second. I used to be quite confident growing up. I did well with ponies and at school. No big family problems or dramas in life, but I've always been shy. I can find people hard work; that's probably why I prefer animals because they're themselves with no ulterior motives." She paused, staring straight out at the road ahead of her.

"And there was this time, I remember, when I was around fifteen, I did a Young Farmer's public speaking competition. My team nominated me to be the speaker. Obviously, I didn't want to do it, but they said it would be good for me. If I could speak in public, I'd stop being so shy as there's nothing worse for an introvert than public speaking. They were probably right, and had good intentions, but on the night, when I stood up to speak…I just couldn't. I totally froze. All I could see was everyone staring at me, and all I could think was, *they think I'm an idiot. And the longer I stand here without saying anything, the more of an idiot I seem to be.* So, I ran away. I just had to get out of there."

"You hated being the centre of attention with everyone looking at you?" Amber understood completely how that felt and recognised Caroline's feelings as her own.

"Yep. And I still do. University was a struggle. I was desperate to come home. But I want to work in conservation, and I needed to get my degree to do it, so I had to stick it out. Being a student wasn't really 'me', though. I'm doing a Masters in Conservation Biology through distance learning now and I much prefer it. And when I'm qualified, I hope to spend most of my time working with animals and saving them from humans."

That night when Amber was in bed, after relaying the events of the day over and over to her parents, she thought about what Caroline had said. Now that she knew more about her, she could see that they were so alike. But although Caroline was quiet and worried about what people thought of her, she was brilliant. Why couldn't she see that? It reminded Amber of something JoJo had said to her – something about her quiet determination being inspirational. She often thought about it. Her parents had said something similar too, but she hadn't believed them. She thought they were just trying to make her feel better about being pathetic. But maybe people did see something positive in her like she did in Caroline. *But what does Caroline think of me? Does she like me?*

The thought gripped Amber and wouldn't let go. *Does she just think I'm a kid with nothing about me? I've helped her today, but Georgia can be helpful, and I still find her annoying. Does Caroline find me annoying?*

From then on, Amber knew that she had to find a way to impress Caroline. She needed to stop asking for her help with problems and show her that she could be independent, strong and resourceful. But what could she do? Amber lay awake, waiting for a brilliant idea to occur to her before sleep closed her mind. But sleep came before any idea, brilliant or otherwise.

# - Eleven -

# Day Dreaming

As soon as she woke the next morning, Amber was straight on her phone. It was still early, but her mind had been sorting through things she could do to impress Caroline all night. Some had been highly dramatic and played through her dreams like movies. In one, she had given Caroline some last-minute insight into how to ride a tricky fence at a competition. Every other rider was having problems with it, but Caroline followed Amber's advice and ended up winning. It was glorious. In another, she'd been with Caroline at some sort of awards ceremony. Caroline had been declared the winner of something and invited to the stage to accept her award and make a speech. But she froze. The spotlight was on her, and people were clapping, expecting her to get up and move. But she couldn't. Her eyes were wide with terror, and the look she gave Amber said, 'Help me.' And so Amber had gone up to the stage, the beam of the light hot on the back of her neck. She'd taken the award and made an impassioned speech about how fantastic Caroline was, which earned a standing ovation from the crowd. When she'd returned to the table, Caroline had embraced her in a tight hug and squeezed her 'til she could hardly breathe. Heavenly.

They were wonderful dreams, but not realistic. As Amber's eyes opened, her final dream was fresh in her mind: it was herself riding to victory on a new horse with Caroline cheering her on.

That was something she could do. She needed to forget about Darcy and start looking for a new horse. A good one. Not one that she needed help with, like Molly. One that she could train, with Caroline, and take eventing with her. They could go to competitions together and be a team, supporting each other.

She knew that she still had Honey, a great pony, but she wasn't going to take Amber to the next level. And, if she was honest, she'd liked the idea of being the first one of her friends to graduate from ponies onto horses. For her to be the one leading the way in something had seemed so novel and out of the ordinary; it was exciting. If Amber could find the perfect horse, she could impress her friends and Caroline at the same time. And she could stop worrying about making a fool of herself in front of Elisha too.

Hours later, she was still in bed, and her phone was out of charge. She could hear her parents moving around and knew she had to get up too. They were picking Georgia up on their way to the stables again, and she was going to ride out with her on Honey. Amber trudged down the stairs and plonked herself heavily in a kitchen chair, rubbing her screen-tired eyes. As she plugged her phone in, she sighed heavily. Stig jumped into her lap the moment she sat down and started butting her with his black and white head. She stroked his sleek black fur automatically while reaching for the cereal.

"That was a big sigh for first thing in the morning," Mrs Anderson, already seated at the table, observed. "I hope it's not because you're grumpy about riding with Georgia. I know you're still disappointed about Darcy, but it's not Georgia's fault. You shouldn't take it out on her."

"No, it's not Georgia. I've just been looking on horses for sale websites, and there aren't any."

"There aren't any?"

"Well, none that are suitable," she said through a mouthful of milk and cereal and had to catch a dribble leaking down her chin with her spoon. "They're all either too far away or too expensive."

Mrs Anderson gave a small smile and pulled a piece of folded paper out of her dressing gown pocket. "Yes, it would've been nice to find something locally, and then you could have tried it a few times to make sure it was right. But we've looked and asked around and haven't found anything in the county either. But we have found these." She unfolded the paper and passed it across the table to Amber.

Amber took it and saw that it was a printed sheet containing two horse adverts. The top one was a beautiful chestnut with a darker brown mane and tail. He was a 15.2hh middleweight and looked fantastic. The second one was smaller – the ad said he was 15hh, but in the picture, he looked like a pony. He was a bay roan like Emily's Pink, but without the Mohican mane. He was pretty, but her eyes were drawn to the top horse. He was by far the more impressive looking of the two.

"They're not local, but they're both inbetween Manchester and Liverpool, so we could take a day and go and see them both. What do you think?"

Amber reread the adverts. The chestnut was a nine-year-old. He was described as kind and good to do in every way. He hadn't done any competing but had loose jumped a metre ten and showed 'good potential'. The roan was eleven and was a 'good allrounder.'

She felt a fizz of excitement bound through her as she looked over at her mother and nodded.

Phone calls were made, and arrangements put in place to go and see the two geldings on Thursday. In the meantime, Amber rode out with Georgia on the Fell ponies. Her mood had lifted, and she listened patiently to Georgia telling her all about the history of the Fell pony breed. Since getting Pearl on loan, she'd become fixated on the pony, and whenever she wasn't at the yard, she was reading and researching everything about the breed. Georgia ignored the fact that Pearl wasn't a pure-bred Fell pony and was becoming an oracle on the Cumbrian breeders. She knew all the prefixes and could recite the breed standards off by heart.

Amber only half listened, giving Georgia an occasional "mmm" when it sounded like she was waiting for a response. She wasn't fully concentrating as she was thinking about the prospect of her new horse. It would be nice to have a bay roan, as then she'd be matching with Emily. It'd be cool to do pairs or team competitions together with twin horses, but the chestnut was the one getting the most air time in her daydreams. He was a proper horse, and she loved imagining how it would feel to ride him. She pictured herself going out eventing with Caroline and Lady and being at the same level as them. She also imagined how it would feel to ride out with JoJo on Merry and be above her, looking down. The simple idea of being higher than JoJo gave her a guilty pleasure. Amber didn't like to admit it, but it would be nice to feel that she was being looked up to for once.

"You're *not* listening. Amber!" Georgia's indignant tone of voice cut through her reverie.

"Sorry, I am."

"What was I saying then?"

"Er…" Amber cast around, trying to recall what Georgia had been saying when she was last paying attention.

"See! I knew you weren't. I might as well be talking to myself!"

"Sorry, Georgia, I'm just a bit distracted at the moment."

"Are you thinking about boys?" Georgia asked randomly.

"WHAT? No, of course not!" Georgia's sudden switch of topic surprised her. "Why would I be thinking about boys?"

"You're thirteen. My auntie told me that thirteen-year-old girls are *obsessed* with boys. Do you have a boyfriend?"

"NO."

"Do you fancy anyone?" Georgia asked, a sly expression creeping across her features.

"No!" Amber blushed as an image of Daniel, Caroline's younger brother, flashed into her mind. "But I suppose I *was* thinking about boys in a way – geldings." She went on, swiftly changing the subject, hoping Georgia hadn't noticed her red cheeks. Before the girl had a chance to ask her anything more, she launched into a description of the two geldings she'd be trying on Thursday. "And," Amber finished off, as they rode back up the farm track towards the yard, "I'm really pleased to be riding Honey again. She has to wear this mesh mask to keep light out of her eye for a bit longer, but it's so much better now, and it won't be long until she's fully healed and back to normal. It's such a relief."

Now that the conversation had returned to Georgia's favourite topic, she was fully distracted from asking any further nosey and embarrassing questions. Amber sighed with relief as Georgia launched into a monologue about the science of equine vision. But as they dismounted in the yard, Amber tensed. Daniel came out of the farmhouse in his overalls. He gave them a cheery wave before climbing up into a waiting tractor. Amber's heart did a little flip, and heat rose in her cheeks again. She glanced furtively at Georgia but was relieved to see that the girl hadn't noticed. Her head was covered by the saddle flap as she loosened Pearl's girth, and she was locked into her own world again.

*Phew,* Amber thought. *I'm glad she didn't see that.* She led Honey back to the stable. Her thoughts of new horses were replaced by the image of Daniel waving at her. It made her smile.

# - Twelve -

## Amber's Next Move

"This is Fox," the woman said, leading the horse, who was ready and tacked up, from his stable. Amber almost squealed with anticipation. He was absolutely gorgeous and named Fox – which was also the name of her favourite event horse, Zero Fox – it was an omen. He was meant to be hers.

His deep chestnut coat gleamed over his perfect physique. His neck was well-muscled, he was short-coupled and perfectly in proportion. He had two white socks on his hind legs and a thin white stripe running down his face. His darker mane and tail were both perfectly pulled, and he'd been groomed to show standard. Even his tack all looked new and expensive. He was like one of the horses used as a model in equestrian catalogues. Amber couldn't wait to ride him.

First, they watched one of his lady owners ride him in the arena while the other filled them in on the situation. Amber was too focused on watching Fox to pay proper attention to her, but she caught something about how they both shared Fox and had their days each when they rode and looked after him. Neither of them wanted to compete, they just hacked mainly, but the woman speaking to them had a new job and was moving away. The other lady couldn't afford to keep him by herself and didn't have the time to see him every day, so they'd decided to sell him. *Why didn't the other woman see if she could find another sharer?* flickered through Amber's mind, but she chased it away. It was good that he was being sold. That way, he could be hers.

"Would you like a ride on him now, Amber?" the lady riding him asked as she pulled up in front of the Andersons.

Amber didn't need to be asked twice. She fastened her hat strap and hurried to the mounting block where Fox was being held, ready for her.

Her first impression was that he seemed huge. Although only a hand taller than Molly, he felt so much bigger. His shoulders were massive, and his neck was much thicker than she was used to.

When she'd watched Fox being ridden around the arena, he'd looked good, but being on board didn't live up to her expectations. He was quite lazy and needed a lot of leg to get him going and keep him moving. After riding Molly for the last fifteen months, she realised how accustomed to a forward going mount she'd become. Fox was more like a bigger version of Pearl. She had to work hard to get him to canter around the arena, but it must've looked okay to everyone because soon the riding lady asked if she'd like a jump put up.

"We don't jump," the woman with Mr and Mrs Anderson told them, "but we've been loose jumping him, and he seems to really enjoy it."

Mr Anderson entered the arena to help drag some wings and poles into position so that Amber had a cross pole and a straight down the two long sides of the arena. They were set to around seventy centimetres.

"Come on then, boy." Amber clicked to Fox and urged him into a canter. He did perk up a bit when he realised there were now jumps to do, but he still lacked impulsion. By the time Amber had jumped them a few times, up to around eighty centimetres, her legs were aching from pushing him on.

"Obviously, he's not very experienced at jumping," the non-riding lady said from the side of the arena where she'd been watching Amber. "He'd need some lessons and more practice, but he's nice and safe and doesn't rush at the fences, which is good, isn't it?"

Amber nodded politely. It was a fact that he certainly did not rush his fences.

"Would you like to take him for a little hack?"

Amber was given directions for a short circular ride she could go on while the adults went for a cuppa in the yard's tea room. Pleased to have a rest, she set off. Fox went very nicely at first, albeit quite slowly, but after a little while, Amber detected a slight change in his way of walking. His back end felt like it dipped and swung slightly as if he was throwing one of his hind legs out to the side. She turned in the saddle to look but couldn't see him doing anything noticeable. *Maybe I've imagined it,* she thought. *Maybe he's just got a different action that I'm not used to. Maybe it's a horse thing.*

When she got back to the yard, she mentioned it to the two women.

"Oh, don't worry about that," said the one who did all the talking. "He'll just be doing that because he's not used to you."

Fox was returned to his stable, where Amber admired him again as he was untacked and groomed. He really was the most handsome horse. Everyone would be dazzled if she turned up at shows with him. Yes, he was a bit quiet, but at least that meant he'd be safe. She wouldn't feel worried about what he was going to do next, like she had with Molly, and maybe he'd perk up a bit when ridden in company, rather than by himself. And there was the option of trying some different feeds to see if that would give him more energy. They'd tried that with Pearl once – they'd given her oats before a show, hoping it might pep her up a bit. But she'd been the same old Pearl, with added flatulence. It had been so embarrassing as she'd farted all the way round her show jumping, as slowly as ever. But now Amber knew there were equine nutritionists who could advise on the perfect feed for your horse. She was sure that Fox could be livened up a bit, one way or another.

"Well, he was a lovely horse, wasn't he?" Mrs Anderson said as they drove out of the yard in the direction of the second horse.

"He was awesome," Amber agreed, pushing her doubts away and focusing on Fox's glamourous appearance.

They were relieved to find the second venue. It was a riding school, but not like the Pine Tree Riding School they were used to, located in the middle of forestry and fells. This one was in the middle of a residential area, and Mr Anderson had been convinced their car's satnav was taking them to the wrong place until they saw the sign for Mason Lane Stables. The sign was pillar box red in colour with the writing in large white capitals. It was placed on the wall of what looked like a garage. There appeared to be a driveway sandwiched between the garage and a house.

"Down here?" Mr Anderson asked incredulously. "It looks like we'll be driving into someone's back garden!"

He inched the car down the narrow driveway, passing the house and its back garden. The drive twisted around and passed more houses before opening out into a moderately sized yard. There was nothing fancy about it, but it was tidy and well-kept with a serene, professional air. Hanging baskets full of pansies were spaced out along the grey brick walls, and all of the stable doors were painted bright red. It looked like the owners were doing everything they could to brighten up what could have been a pretty drab, ordinary yard. An antique-looking wall clock hung from an ornate bracket completing the picture.

"Hi, we're here to view a horse?" Mrs Anderson called to a girl carrying water buckets across the yard as they climbed out of the car. The girl tilted her head towards the clock but didn't put the buckets down.

"He's over there, in the end stable. I'll just go and tell Yvonne that you're here."

Amber approached the stable and looked inside, but it was gloomy, and she couldn't see its occupant clearly. Sliding the door's bolt back, she opened it and stepped inside.

"Hello boy," she said to the small horse inside. She was surprised to see he was rugged despite it being a warm summer's day. The horse turned his head towards her with his ears pinned flat to his head, and his nostrils flared. He shook his head savagely at her and swished his tail menacingly. Amber staggered back out through the door and closed it behind her.

"He's not very friendly," Amber stated the obvious to her parents as they all took a step away from the horse's stable.

"Oh, I'm so sorry!" A woman with short, curly blonde hair scuttled across to them. She wore riding clothes but looked clean and smart. She clearly wasn't part of the mucking out team. "Jessie should have sent you to the office to find me, not straight over to Rusty's stable. I see he hasn't made a great first impression."

"I'm Yvonne," she said, shaking hands with everyone, "and I see you've already met the lovely Rusty. Before you get put off by his stable manners, or lack of, I just want to let you know a few things." She sighed and entered the stable, putting a head collar on the horse and leading him out into the yard. Once there, he pricked his ears and looked with interest at the goings-on. Suddenly, he looked quite pretty. It seemed like Mr Hyde had been left in the stable, and this was Dr Jekyll.

"He's grumpy in the stable as he's protective of his food. If he thinks you're going to take his haynet off him, he'll defend it. And the poor boy has reason to behave like that," Yvonne removed Rusty's rug and placed it over his stable door, "as you can see."

"Gosh, he's thin, isn't he?" Mrs Anderson blurted out. The little horse was very narrow with a tiny chest. His hip bones protruded through his roan coat, and his ribs were visible.

"That's the polite version," Yvonne agreed. "He'll always be a slim build - we've no breeding for him, but I think he's probably Arab or thoroughbred crossed with a pony breed – but he's been neglected. A client here reported him to us. The poor thing was tethered on a bit of common ground on one of the estates. He didn't seem to have any water, and he was constantly being tormented by kids, you know, throwing stones at him and that kind of thing. We managed to find the owner and got them to accept an offer for him, rather than be reported for neglect, and we brought him here." She smoothed her hand along his neck.

"And apart from the fact he's protective of his food, and he's not keen on kids, he's a lovely little horse. He's nice to ride, but he's suspicious of new people. With his past, I don't blame him. We just thought that this set-up –

the riding school – isn't what's best for him. He'd be better off with a one-to-one relationship with a rider and a team of people who are constant, that he can get used to. I'd really like to see him in a good home with people who understand his behaviour and don't punish him for it. I think with kindness and patience, he'll be a lovely boy for someone, won't you, my little rust bucket?" She stroked his muzzle gently. Rusty showed no aggression.

"Would you like to see him ridden?"

Rusty, they soon learned, wasn't keen on being saddled either and gnashed his teeth just like Molly when his girth was done up, but he kept his teeth to himself. When ridden, he went well for the young male rider who was asked to show him off to them. He moved forward nicely and popped over a few fences quite happily.

"Your turn." The lad smiled as he slipped off Rusty's back and handed the reins to Amber. "There's nothing I need to tell you. He's straight forward and forgiving. Enjoy."

***

"So, we've a decision to make," Mr Anderson said as they headed back up the M6 towards home. "They're both lovely horses, but we can only have one of them, so will it be Rusty or Foxy?"

"It's Fox, Dad. Not Foxy."

"It's a tough one, and it's up to you, Amber, but I enjoyed watching you on Rusty," Mrs Anderson chipped in. "You looked happy."

Amber had to admit that her mother was right. When she'd started riding Rusty, she'd immediately discovered that the boy's appraisal of the horse was correct. He was easy. There was no strange, unfamiliar feeling like there had been with Fox. No sense of 'it'll take a while to get used to you.' He didn't feel like a new horse. He felt just like Molly. It was like she'd known him for ages. Unlike Fox, he hadn't needed to be constantly urged to go forward. He was keen and responsive, but obedient. He reacted immediately to every aid she gave him. His appearance had made her expect him to feel fragile and wooden, but he was well-schooled. He was pony-ish, but his paces were surprisingly powerful. Even in walk, he was on a mission. When she'd started jumping him, it had been so smooth and uncomplicated, the young lad had put one up to a metre and invited her to try it. She would never have imagined that she'd be confident enough to put a new horse at a fence that size, but she didn't hesitate. Amber was so comfortable with Rusty, she knew he'd jump it for her. And he did. Easily. Clearly, someone had once spent time with this horse, for he knew his job well. Amber couldn't understand how he could have ended up as a neglect case.

By the time she'd finished in the arena and took him for a hack to cool off, she was grinning all over her face. Rusty made her feel the same way Darcy had: hopeful, optimistic and relaxed. As she slouched along on a long rein with her feet out of the stirrups, it struck her how long it had been since she'd felt this relaxed while riding. On the Fell ponies, yes, but occasions like this with Molly were few and far between.

And now she had to choose.

She knew she could have a lot of fun with Rusty. But she could just imagine the look on Elisha Templeton's face when she saw him. The words she'd say echoed in Amber's mind. She could hear Elisha's voice as if she was sitting right there next to her: *scrawny, skeleton, sympathy case*... Whereas Fox looked like a champion. Everyone, including Elisha, would be impressed with him. He might've been a bit sluggish today, but maybe he was just bored? He didn't seem to have a very exciting life. Maybe if he started being taken to shows and having some gallops in the forestry and on the fells, he'd brighten up a bit. And he could always be given more energy from feed.

Amber did feel sorry for Rusty. He'd had a hard time and been mistreated. Her heart went out to him, but there'd be somebody else who'd give him a good home and a nice life. It didn't have to be her.

And so, the pendulum of decision stopped swinging. Amber's mind was made up.

"Fox," she said. "I choose Fox."

# - Thirteen -

# A Waiting Game

Amber gulped her orange juice so fast, she almost choked. "But I want to go with Dad and Caroline to pick up Fox!"

"Well, I'm afraid you can't. It's Grandma's birthday on Sunday, and we've already arranged to take her out to that hotel she likes in Keswick for afternoon tea. You know how much she'll be looking forward to it."

"Can't you just take her for tea?"

"Amber." Mrs Anderson plonked the iron down onto the ironing board heavily. Steam hissed out of it, as if it too was annoyed with her. "Your grandma expects to see you and your cousins on her birthday. You're all so busy now, the only time she ever sees you all together is on her birthday and at Christmas. So, you're going." She picked the iron up and started vigorously pushing it up and down the leg of a pair of jeans. "You won't be missing out on anything. They're literally going to drive down to the yard, load Fox up and come all the way back again. You know how bored you get travelling, and this will be ultra-boring – creeping along the motorway in Caroline's cattle truck. It'll take hours. We'll go and do the afternoon tea, then come to the yard. You can be there to unload him and settle him into his stable for the night. Okay?"

"Well, I suppose it'll have to be." Amber flounced off to her bedroom to show that she still disapproved of the plan, although really, she knew it made sense. She did find travelling mind-numbingly dull, and it would've broken a lifelong family tradition if she didn't see her grandma on her birthday. But Amber was twitching with excitement over the arrival of her new horse and didn't want to miss out on a second of it.

Fox's owners were keen for him to be picked up on Sunday as it meant they could both be there to wave him off. Plus, the Anderson's pony-sized trailer was too small for Fox, so Caroline had offered to drive down to Liverpool in her lorry with Mr Anderson to pick him up, to save them having to organise a horse transporter. She didn't have a competition to go to with Lady, and she needed a break from her degree work, so she was happy to volunteer. Amber had wanted to be there to introduce Caroline to her new horse and see her reaction when she saw him for the first time. But instead, she had to put on some nice clothes and go and endure a prim and proper afternoon tea with her grandparents, auntie and cousins – Liam and Harvey – and her mother in a posh hotel. Normally, she looked forward to it. The cakes were always lovely, and it was a treat. But this time, she knew she'd be too distracted to enjoy it.

Sunday turned out to be a cloudy day, with grey clouds that threatened rain. Mr Anderson left the house to head to Shaw Farm with a packed lunch and a head full of instructions to text Amber to let her know what was going on. She wanted a picture of Fox with Caroline. She wanted to see him in his travelling gear.

"Make sure you remember to put the tail bandage on. Do you know how to do it? Not too tight, but not too loose either. Maybe you'd better ask Caroline to do it." She wanted updates of how he was travelling and where they were so she could make sure she was at the yard waiting for them when they arrived.

"Don't forget, will you? Is your phone charged?" Amber fussed as he opened the kitchen door to head out.

"Yes, my dear, now go and enjoy your day. Wish your grandma a happy birthday from me, and if anyone is too full to eat all their cakes, ask someone to put them in a box for you, and you can bring me some back. I love their fruit cake, and the Victoria sponge is always delicious too."

"You can have my fruit cake. I never eat it. Here..." She handed him a plastic bag containing some apples and carrots. "These are for Fox from me. You can use them to help load him if you need. He's probably not used to going in a lorry as they don't take him anywhere, so—"

Mr Anderson cut her off by leaning forward and giving her a kiss on the forehead. He took the bag and said, "I'm sure we'll manage. I've got the horse whisperer with me, so it'll all be fine. Now, go and have a nice time, and I'll see you later." He closed the door after him, leaving Amber to go and find something suitable to wear for the day. She doubted that Liam and Harvey would have to put much thought into it. It was easy for boys – decent trousers and a shirt. But since getting ponies, Amber's only interest in clothes was in breeches, riding tops and gilets. Whenever she wasn't in school uniform, she lived in riding gear. Did she even have anything nice that would still fit?

The afternoon tea dragged on. Amber barely ate anything. She couldn't concentrate and perched on the end of her seat, her right leg jiggling with impatience. She answered the obligatory questions from her grandparents – how was she, how were the ponies, how were the school holidays – but once the adults starting speaking to each other, Amber zoned out and wondered what was going on with her dad, Caroline, and Fox. When she was younger, she'd have played in the hotel's garden with Liam and Harvey. They used to be like brothers to her as they'd often spent a lot of the school holidays together with their grandparents while their parents were at work. But now they were older – Liam was fifteen and Harvey, twelve - there was no playing. She had nothing in common with them anymore, and the three of them sat around like spare parts, each looking as uncomfortable as the other.

Amber surreptitiously slid her phone out of her shoulder bag and pinged off a silent text to her dad demanding an update. They were bound to have reached

Liverpool by now. Why wasn't he letting her know what was going on? Her right leg jiggled faster, and she sighed loudly, earning a look of warning from her mother. Amber knew she was being rude with her restless manner, but she couldn't help it. She just didn't want to be there.

Eventually, as 4pm approached, the adults began to signal that it was time to go home. Relieved that she could finally escape, she gave her grandparents and her auntie a big hug as they left their table in the hotel's conservatory.

"Send us some pictures of the new horse, Amber," her grandma said, waving her new birthday smart phone at her. "I need to practise using this thing. One of you three young uns will probably have to give me a lesson next time we see you." She indicated Amber and her cousins. "You know where we live. It'd be nice to see more of you."

As Amber gave her a goodbye hug, she said, "I know you've been itching to get away and see your new horse Amber, so we'll let you go."

"Sorry, Grandma." Amber squeezed her grandma's slim frame tightly. "I'm on another planet today."

"It's alright, love. You go and meet your new boy. What's his name? Socks?"

Amber laughed, “No, it’s Fox, Grandma. Like the animal.”

“Oh! Sorry, I think I’m going deaf.”

“It was lovely to see you both.” Amber put her arms around her grandad. After hugging her, he opened his huge hand to show her three white cubes of sugar he’d sneaked out of the sugar bowl on their table. He slid them into her palm.

“One each for t’ponies and for’t new lad, tha’knows,” he said in his unique voice; a blend of his native Danish accent combined with the west coast Cumbrian dialect he’d picked up while working in the pits. “We’ll ‘ave to come and watch you at a show with him. It’s ower lang since we’ve been to one.”

“Yes,” Grandma agreed, “the gymkhanos are a nice day out. Let us know when you’re going to one, and we’ll come along.”

“It’s a gymkhana, Grandma, not a gymkhano. But nobody really calls them that anymore. We just say show.”

At long last, Amber was able to scramble into the house, get changed, clip Kasper's lead onto his collar and get back into the car to head to the yard.

"Hurry up, Mum," she urged, "or they'll be there before us. Why hasn't Dad sent me any messages or replied to mine?" She tapped at her phone screen, checking texts and WhatsApp but finding nothing.

"Keep your hair on Amber, you know what Dad's like with messages. He doesn't check his phone, and if he does get a message, his replies are only ever 'yes, no or okay.' Everything will be fine."

The journey to the yard seemed to take much longer than the actual half an hour that passed. But when they finally pulled into the yard, there was no sign of Caroline's lorry, and Molly's vacant stable was still empty. Amber paced up and down the yard, firing off texts to her dad, 'where are you?', 'how long will you be?', 'is everything alright? Please can you reply????' But her phone remained silent. No answering messages beeped.

Worn out from the day-long anticipation, Amber and Mrs Anderson sat on the farmyard wall to wait while Kasper sniffed about on the lane. Amber swung her legs and bumped the heels of her yard boots against the stones. It was impossible to keep still with all the nervous energy that crackled through her.

"Did you hear that?" Amber's head snapped up as she heard a distant clank of metal. "They're here!"

She jumped off the wall and stood in the middle of the lane until Caroline's lorry appeared from around a bend, tilting slightly in the potholes that the large vehicle couldn't avoid. At long last, the lorry crept into the yard and before Caroline and her dad were even out of the cab, Amber was lowering the ramp to see her new horse.

"Amber, no. Wait! There's something I need to -" Mr Anderson clambered down from the cab and tried to reach his daughter before she ascended the ramp and saw inside the lorry. But it was too late. Amber was already there, staring at the horse. It wasn't Fox.

# - Fourteen -

# The Wrong Horse

“What the - ?” Amber gasped as she took in the image in front of her. Instead of seeing the sight she’d expected, something else completely met her eyes. She closed them and squeezed them tightly, her whole face scrunching up as she willed it to be some sort of dream or mirage. She prayed that when she opened them again, it wouldn’t be true. But it didn’t work. When she opened her eyes, it was still Rusty she saw in Caroline’s lorry, not Fox.

“What…why…?” she spluttered, unable to formulate words that made sense.

“Er…yeah. Slight change of plan,” Mr Anderson replied sheepishly.

“*Slight change of plan*? It’s a different blinking horse!” Amber screeched, her words coming freely now.

"Where's Fox? You were going to pick *Fox* up. Why've you brought the wrong horse?"

Mr Anderson climbed up the ramp and moved Amber gently out of the way so he could open the partition and lead Rusty out. "Let's get him out and put him in his stable. He's had a long journey. Then I'll tell you all about it."

Amber barely noticed Caroline hovering around in the background as she watched her father lead Rusty into the stable she'd prepared for Fox. Amber couldn't believe this was happening. Her mind and body were numb. Her mother had to put her arm around her and walk her forwards to get her moving from where she stood, rooted to the spot beside the lorry ramp.

After Mr Anderson removed Rusty's travel boots and head collar, he left the horse to his hay net and began his story. Amber listened wordlessly, still wrapped in her mother's arms.

"It was quiet on the motorway, so we got there about half an hour earlier than we expected," he began. "When we pulled into the yard, we could see that Fox was in the arena being lunged. Caroline pointed out that it seemed a strange thing to be doing – working a horse right before it's about to travel. It jogged my memory that he was already tacked up in his stable when we went to see him. I didn't think anything of it at the time, but seeing them working Fox before we arrived made me wonder if they'd done the same thing before you came to try him. I remembered you saying something about him having a bit of a funny action when you rode him. I mentioned it to Caroline, and she was immediately suspicious."

Amber's eyes swivelled towards Caroline, who had been standing quietly on the sidelines. She blushed as she realised it was her turn to speak.

"I...yeah...something just seemed off. The lady lunging him seemed in a bit of a panic when she saw us arriving early and tried to explain it away. She said she was just giving him a leg stretch while his stable was mucked out. We didn't say anything about it, but I started to give him a bit of a check over."

"She didn't like that." Mr Anderson interrupted. "And the other woman came dashing out of the stable asking what we were doing. I said my knowledgeable companion here was just giving him a once over, and she went mad! She started shouting that the sale was agreed and we couldn't start doing a vetting now. I said it wasn't a vetting, but then Caroline basically started doing just that – holding his legs up for those flexion test things."

"And that's when we found it," Caroline came back in. "I'm sorry, Amber but he was lame. He wasn't too bad in his front legs, but his hinds were very stiff, especially his right hind. I think he might have bone spavin in at least one, if not both of his hocks." She noticed Amber staring blankly at her and explained further. "It's osteoarthritis – a degenerative joint disease. He's only young to have it, but he was slightly cow hocked, so maybe his confirmation has contributed. Anyway, it's not something you want in a horse you're buying to compete on."

"So…based on that, I told them we wouldn't be taking him." Mr Anderson looked at Amber, trying to read her reaction, but she was stony faced. Even her expressive left eyebrow gave nothing away. "We got out of there pretty quick after that. They were screaming at me for being a timewaster."

"But I'm pretty sure they knew there was something not right with him," Caroline said in support of Mr Anderson. "They might not have had a diagnosis, but they definitely knew he was stiff and were trying to loosen him up so that he didn't look lame when we came to load up.

I think they were trying to hide it from you and must've been delighted when you agreed to buy him without getting him vetted."

"I know. We should have." Mrs Anderson spoke for the first time. "But he looked so strong and healthy, we thought there couldn't be anything wrong with him. But we don't have your experience. We should have made sure. I suppose we were rushing. Again." She shook her head. "So how come the wee fella is here then?" she asked.

"Well. As we set off driving back, I told Caroline about the other horse we'd tried. She liked the sound of him, and instead of coming all the way back home with an empty lorry, she said we might as well go and take a look at him if he was still available. So, I rang Yvonne, and she said he was still there, so we went. They couldn't have been more helpful. That same young lad rode him again."

"And I even had a little go on him," interjected Caroline, "even though I'm really too big for him. And I thought he was lovely. So, then we trotted him up, I checked his legs and did the flexion tests, and he was fine.

Obviously, I couldn't listen to his heart and lungs, but he was certainly a lot sounder than the other horse."

"So, I had a chat with Yvonne, and she was brilliant. I've given her a deposit for him, and she's let me take him on a two-week trial."

"Which is amazing," Caroline joined in, "as nobody usually lets you take a horse away on trial. Not unless you're local and they know you."

"Yes. So, I thought there was nothing to lose. You can see how you get on with him in these last two weeks of the holidays, we can get him properly vetted and if there are any problems, we can take him back. The fact that she's so open and honest makes me feel much happier about it. So… yeah, that's the story. What do you think?"

Amber peered over the stable door at the skinny horse attacking his haynet. She'd heard the story and understood the logic, but still, disappointment and anger seethed inside her. Amber bit her lip, not wanting to release any words that she'd regret later. "I don't believe this," was all she said as she turned her back on them all and walked away.

Amber knew it would come across as a sulk, but she'd rather them think that than know the truth. The telltale burn in her throat signalled that tears were searching for a release as she dived into the cool darkness of the tack room to hide.

She'd allowed herself to dream again. Her hopes of being as good as her friends, of impressing Caroline, of silencing Elisha had been wide awake at the thought of Fox being her horse. He was going to help her move forward. Molly hadn't been a good choice in the game of ponies. Their time together had been like snakes and ladders; as soon as they made progress, something happened to send them backwards.

She was determined not to go backwards anymore. Yet here was Rusty. It felt like checkmate. Yes, he was on trial and could go back, but for now, she was stuck with him. Trapped like a king in check with no way out.

# - Fifteen -

# The Right Horse

Owing to his unique shape, Yvonne had let Rusty's saddle come with him during his trial to make sure he would be comfortable. With his small head, Honey's bridle could be let out slightly to fit him, meaning that Amber could start riding Rusty straight away. The last couple of days she'd hacked out on him, and Amber had to admit, she'd enjoyed her rides. Rusty had amazing stamina. He left the yard like he was on a mission and kept up the pace all the way round. He came back from a ride feeling as fresh as a daisy. And he seemed to enjoy being ridden. He was much sweeter in the stable after a ride, and showed no signs of the grumpiness he displayed when approached before exercise.

The day Georgia met him for the first time, Rusty hadn't held back in showing his hatred of her. As soon as she'd entered his stable, ready to greet him enthusiastically, he'd snaked his head. With ears flat back and nostrils flared, his body language left the girl in no doubt that he was saying, "Stay away from me," as loudly as possible.

"Don't take it personally. He's horrible and hates everyone, but you'll probably be enemy number one as he detests kids the most," Amber told her, explaining Rusty's past and how he'd been terrorised by children. Georgia's reaction to this had surprised Amber. She'd expected the girl to back out of the stable, resolving to keep well away from him. But she forgot that Georgia was Georgia.

"Poor boy. He's probably not horrible. He just thinks he has to stick up for himself and frighten people away before they get a chance to hurt him. I can help to cure his fear of kids." And with a new mission set firmly in her sights, Georgia ignored the increasing signs of agitation Rusty displayed and inched slowly closer to the horse. Rusty snapped his teeth menacingly, but undeterred, Georgia produced a carrot from her pocket and held it out to him. Rusty's ears flicked forward as he spied the treat, and he extended his lips towards the end Georgia pointed towards him. He curled his lips around it with surprising gentleness and sucked it into his mouth like a piece of spaghetti, crunching it happily for a second, before turning back into Mr Nasty, warning Georgia to keep back. The girl made no attempt to get closer to him and kept her distance, whispering to him, all about a book she'd been reading about a boy who was bullied because his face didn't look the same as other children. Eventually, Rusty sighed and turned back to his haynet. He kept one ear locked on to the girls standing in his stable, but ignored them as far as possible.

"You're wasting your time," Amber grumped. "He's just a misery guts."

"Not necessarily," argued Georgia, using her favourite catchphrase. Amber's hackles rose whenever she heard it. "He's probably just worried and anxious and misunderstood, like the boy in the story I read. But you're lucky. He's your horse now, and you can be kind to him and show him how lovely people can actually be, and he'll love you and become your best friend ever." Georgia's voice caught at the end, and she stopped speaking abruptly. Amber regarded her closely. Did she have tears in her eyes? She remembered something Georgia's dad had said about her not having many friends.

Amber was making no effort to connect with Rusty. She certainly didn't feel lucky to have him, and she hadn't spoken to Caroline since he'd arrived on Sunday, but something about Georgia's response to Rusty thawed her slightly. If the girl hadn't taken an instant dislike to him after that unfriendliest of first meetings, and was prepared to give him a chance, maybe she should try to do the same.

"Do you fancy coming for a ride out with me?" Amber offered.

"Oh yeah!" Georgia immediately brightened and practically skipped off to get Pearl ready.

***

"He's lovely," JoJo said, giving Rusty a rub on the forehead when she saw him for the first time. Amber pursed her lips, wondering if she meant it.

As they'd ridden past Jubilee House, JoJo had been in the yard, loading things into her horsebox. She hadn't yet seen Amber's new horse and quickly vaulted over the closed gate to take a look at him. Away from his stable,

Rusty showed none of the attitude he'd directed at Georgia and let JoJo touch him without complaint.

JoJo knew all about the situation with Fox and Rusty – all her friends had heard her views on the matter several times through WhatsApp, but if she was unimpressed with Amber's new horse, she hid it well.

Amber clenched her teeth. Everyone seemed to like Rusty except her. Unless they were just pretending to be polite. She knew one person who wouldn't pretend or be polite when she clapped eyes on him. Elisha. But, Amber reminded herself, he was only on trial. He could go back before Elisha ever got the chance to see him.

"How come you're loading your lorry on a Wednesday?" Amber asked as JoJo's mum came out of the house carrying pillows and a duvet.

"*Because* we're going down to Warwickshire tomorrow for the Tetrathlon Championship. Thursday is arrive-and-set-up day, and the competition takes place Friday to Sunday." JoJo climbed up onto the gate and sat on the top, her long tanned legs dangling in front of her. "I have told you this several times."

"Oh, yeah, sorry I forgot." Amber felt silly as she remembered that this was why she hadn't seen much of

JoJo recently. When it had been the branch tetrathlon, JoJo hadn't bothered to do any training, just relying on her natural ability to win the small local event. When they'd progressed to Area, she'd done some running practice, and won again. But now she was going to the championship, she realised that talent alone might not be enough. She'd be competing against the best of the best – people who ran and swam for school or county teams. When Amber had suggested that it didn't matter how she did, she should just enjoy the experience, JoJo had scoffed at the idea. She didn't do anything just for the sake of taking part.

And so, since the summer holidays had begun, JoJo had been possessed – running on the fells and forestry tracks, and training in the local pool. Amber didn't imagine she could improve any further, but JoJo was making it her mission.

"I'll be competing against experienced fourteen-year-olds. Some of them will be on National teams. I want to be selected for Nationals next year, so I've got to stand out," JoJo had pointed out during a messaging session with her tetrathlon team mates. Amber had marvelled at how JoJo seemed to thrive when under pressure, while she buckled under it.

"Where's your head at?" JoJo laughed. "Matty's going to Nanna's while we're away, so he's having a last games practice with Flash as we speak." She slid down from the gate and clapped her hands as an idea occurred to her. "Do you two want to go in and help him practise his handovers?"

"Oh…I don't think so," said Amber. "Pearl's really slow at games, and Rusty…well, he's a horse. Horses don't do games. Games is for ponies."

"That doesn't matter." JoJo opened the gate, resisting Amber's attempt to decline the invitation. "It's only playing. And if you want to do Members' Cup at the end of the season on Rusty, you'll have to do everything. Games included."

"Yeah, come on, Amber, let's. I've never done games before. I'd love to try it." Georgia was so animated, Amber couldn't refuse her, much as she wanted to.

"Well, just don't get your hopes up. Rusty won't know what to do and games on Pearl is like a slow-motion replay, so don't expect to be whizzing up and down the bending poles like you're doing Prince Philip Cup."

Georgia kicked Pearl on as JoJo ushered them into the yard. "I don't even know what Prince Philip Cup is, Amber," she said. "Stop being a party pooper and deciding you can't do it before you've even tried."

Amber goggled at Georgia. *She doesn't know what Prince Philip Cup is*. It was the first time she'd ever heard Georgia admit to not knowing something. And she couldn't believe she'd been told off by this little girl in front of JoJo. *Who does she think she is?*

"Well, don't say I didn't warn you," she muttered as she guided Rusty towards the paddock.

***

"I told you so," Georgia gloated an hour later as they rode back up the track to Shaw Farm.

"You told me so? What? You didn't tell me anything."

"Yes, I did! I told you Rusty might be good at games if you gave him a chance."

"No, you didn't. You said I'd decided he couldn't do it before I'd tried."

"Well, doh, that's the same thing, isn't it? And whatever. I was riiiight and you were wrooong!" Amber had never seen Georgia so gleefully manic. Despite being put out that Georgia was right, she couldn't help smiling and leaning forward to give Rusty a pat.

It was true. Amber had assumed the little horse wouldn't know what to do about games, and trying it with him would be pointless. But she'd been wrong. They'd had a fantastic time. Although Pearl moved at a glacial pace, Georgia couldn't have been happier with her first-ever attempt at games. She'd congratulated herself every time she managed to get a flag into its holder, a mug onto a pole (or rather – garden cane) and a sock into a bucket. Amber suspected that, like herself, Georgia probably wasn't a girl who got picked first for sporting teams at school. Matthew was happy to practise handovers and vaulting on, and Amber had discovered that Rusty not only knew about games, but enjoyed them.

It hadn't been obvious straight away. When they began, Rusty shied away from the poles and flags when she'd tried to reach out towards them. But, just as she'd been about to give up, an idea had popped into her head – – to try using her left hand to reach for flags and mugs instead of her right. It worked! As soon as she switched hands, Rusty was perfect. She was able to keep up a continuous canter, using her seat and upper body to steer the horse where she wanted him to go, although he seemed to know exactly what she wanted. When she reached out to grab a flag with her left hand, he didn't shy away, and she was soon doing as well as Matthew on Flash.

"Whooee!" JoJo exclaimed. "He might be fifteen hands, but he's done this before. Someone's trained him for it, somewhere in his past, and I'm sure that person was left-handed."

"Trust me to get a horse that needs to be ridden left-handed," Amber joked.

"I know – now that you're practically left-handed these days, it's like he was meant for you. It's a sign. It was meant to be!" JoJo dropped to her knees and reached up towards the heavens in an attitude of worship. Amber and Georgia giggled at the silly seriousness of her pose.

As Amber sat in front of the TV later that evening, she stared at the screen but couldn't concentrate on what was happening. Her thoughts played back and forth through her head like a game of tennis.

*Rusty is a mistake. I don't want him.*

*He's just on trial and can go back. But JoJo and Georgia like him.*

*Elisha Templeton won't like him.*

*Who cares what she thinks? She doesn't even have her own horse anymore.*

*Rusty is bad-tempered and unfriendly.*

*But that isn't his fault. Maybe, like Georgia says, his manners will improve when he realises no-one is going to hurt him.*

*He doesn't look very impressive.*

*He's a good hack. He's great at games. I'm not scared of him.*

*Could he be the right horse for me, after all?*

# - Sixteen -

## Measuring Up

As always, the final two weeks of the summer holiday sped by like someone had pressed fast forward. At the beginning, the six weeks always seemed as if they would last forever, that each day would stretch and slow to a stroll, so that time could be savoured and enjoyed. But somewhere along the way, the stroll had developed into a sprint, and it would soon be time to return to school.

These holidays hadn't been anything like Amber had hoped for. After the success of the Area Tetrathlon, she'd thought that her problems with Molly were behind her, and she'd been looking forward to a summer full of shows with her. But instead, Molly had gone, and now Rusty was here. In a few days, Amber had to make up her mind whether he was staying or if she wanted to send him back to Liverpool.

It was so hard to decide. Rusty hadn't put a foot wrong whilst being ridden. She'd hacked him out alone and with JoJo after her return from the Tetrathlon Championships and was pleased to find that Merry couldn't hold a candle to Rusty speed-wise. Amber surmised that he must be at least part thoroughbred as his speed was blistering, and he had a real competitive streak. A couple of times, she'd surreptitiously held him back to give JoJo a head start, not wanting her friend to sulk about being beaten every time. But it didn't matter how much she held him back and tried to let Merry stay in the lead. Rusty would just settle into a stride and cruise past her, his ears flat to his head. He didn't fight or feel like he was pulling. It was like he just couldn't help being that fast. Amber imagined that was what it must feel like to be JoJo herself when she ran – overtaking her competitors with such ease. She couldn't deny how secretly pleased it made her that Merry couldn't keep up with Rusty, let alone beat him.

Amber had also jumped him in the Jones' paddock – she'd been keeping out of Caroline's way since Rusty arrived and so hadn't ridden in the jumping paddock at Shaw Farm where Caroline might spot her. Already jumping round a short course of a metre, Amber couldn't believe how quickly she'd clicked with the small horse. After more than a year of struggling to bond with Molly, it was a pleasant surprise to find that she had an immediate connection to Rusty and looked forward to riding him.

On the other hand, he was still protective of his food and continued to be grumpy and threatening in the stable. He never kicked or bit, but Amber didn't trust that he never would and made sure she didn't turn her back on him whilst in the stable with him. It was frustrating that they were a great team when Amber was mounted, but on the ground, they were wary and mistrustful of each other.

And it didn't help that both Chelsea and JoJo had new horses too.

First had been JoJo. She'd arrived back from the Tetrathlon Championships on Sunday with not just Merry in the lorry. A message sent to the tetrathlon team from JoJo at 10.30pm showed a new horse had also been unloaded and was now in the field with Flash, Sam and Merry, getting used to his new home.

He'd been sourced whilst they were down in Warwick. JoJo had had a fantastic time competing in the championship and had sent the team messages every day to appraise them of her progress. On Friday, she'd shot 900 and swam nine lengths and sixteen metres. At the end of the first day, she'd been in fifth place.

"It's amazing," she'd gushed in her update on the first day. "Some of these girls are proper athletes. A lot of them did the Regional competition – which is now called Internationals – earlier in the year. I'm so glad I did some extra training before I came here. We're camping with other people from the Northern England areas. We're all in one section of the camping field, and there's gazebos in the centre of camp for everyone to mingle. They're decorated in pink bunting - pink is the Northern England colour - and fairy lights. It's so cool. Everyone has been really friendly, and they've been looking after me as I'm one of the only people here as an individual. I've seen that awful Keira Thingumy-Watsit AKA 'Bridle Stealer' from the Area comp, and you'll be pleased to know I beat her in the shoot and the swim. I did a bit of psyching her out. It's a funny story. I'll tell you about it when I get back."

Messages had continued to be plentiful. They'd heard all about her cross-country ride on the Saturday – clear but unusually, with time faults. JoJo wasn't as upset about this as Amber would've imagined as the course was 'wicked' apparently – a mini Badminton. It had been full of technical fences, combinations, skinnies on angles and even a jump into the water. "Merry was immense, but it wasn't just a point and kick course. I wanted to make sure she didn't run out at any of the awkward fences, so I made sure I set her up properly for them. It wasted too much time, though, *and* they only allow thirty seconds each for the gate and slip rail. I came in twelve seconds over the time. But loads of people have been congratulating me and saying how well I did for my first time. Apparently, only about a quarter of riders finish with the maximum score for the riding."

The euphoric riding day had been followed up with a zoo-themed fancy dress party which had been 'ace' and went on all night, followed by the run and presentation on Sunday. Her time faults had kept JoJo out of the top ten, but she had come 11$^{th}$ individually, which for a twelve-year-old at her first-ever championship, was a great result.

Eleventh was never going to be enough for JoJo, though. She'd decided that this was her sport and had been advised to try for selection for next year's International team. She'd need to complete in the Northern Triathlon in February, and if successful there, she'd be invited to attend cross-country training for a riding assessment. Merry was a great pony, but only stood at 14.2hh. With her long legs and constant growth, it wouldn't be long before JoJo was too tall for her. So when they'd seen a young horse advertised at the event, they'd decided to go and see him.

They'd viewed him on the Friday after JoJo's swim, and had gone back again on Saturday afternoon after her cross-country to try him again. On Sunday, after the presentation, they'd picked him up and brought him home.

Amber looked at the picture of him JoJo had sent. He was described as piebald, but really he was pretty much black. He had four white stockings and one tiny white strip on his neck and another on his quarters, but otherwise, his body was like black ink. He had a white snip between his nostrils and a tiny, round white star that looked like a moon between his eyes. His breeders had obviously thought it resembled a tiny planet as the horse had been named Pluto. He was anything but a dwarf, though. At only five years old, he was already at least 16.2hh and was no doubt still growing.

He'd been bred to event, but like Merry, displayed a wanton disregard for show jumps. In the cross-country schooling he'd done, however, he was brave, bold and accurate. His owners had wisely decided to advertise him to those involved in the sport of tetrathlon, knowing that competitors needed cross-country specialists. And so here he was to bring on and be ready in the wings for JoJo when she progressed to the senior level of the competition in three years.

Hot on the heels of this exciting news came Chelsea's announcement that Skye had gone to a new home and her new horse was arriving on the coming Saturday. Pictures of him revealed a 16hh rich, red bay. He had no markings at all, but he was far from being plain. Half thoroughbred, half Friesian, he was stunning. He was lean and well-muscled, with a classically arched neck and a long, wavy black mane and forelock. He looked like the type of horse that would be used on a film set. His name was Harris – Coledale Harris Hawk when competing - and

Chelsea took it as a sign that, like her pony Skylark, he was also named after a bird. “We’ll soon be flying over those BE fences,” Chelsea told them. “He’s done some BE80 and 90, so I’ll try and do a few more 90s on him this season and then hopefully move up to 100s next season.”

With those two busy with their new mounts, there was only Emily left who hadn’t yet moved from her pony onto a horse.

“I’ll probably never grow out of Pink with my short stumpy legs,” she joked. “I’ll be keeping my punk rocker ‘til she’s a little old lady!”

As the final weekend of the holidays approached, so did Amber’s deadline. She had to decide what to do about Rusty. She was torn. He *felt* right, but compared to Pluto and Harris, he didn’t *look* right. He was small and thin and just not impressive like her friends’ new horses. She knew she shouldn’t be so shallow as to be using his appearance as a deciding factor, and she’d vowed never to compare her ponies to other people’s again, but she couldn’t help it. Plus the thought of Elisha’s reaction to him if she ever clapped eyes on him constantly plagued her.

"I could take offence that you think he's so visually unappealing, given that he's like Pink's twin," Emily had teased her. "Why don't you take him to Blakefield's trophy show on Bank Holiday Monday and see how he does to help you make your mind up? I'm going, and if they run a pairs scurry, we could do it together, on our pink ponies."

And so it had been decided. Rusty's owner, Yvonne, had agreed to wait for their decision until Monday evening, after the competition. His fate hung in the balance and would be decided by his performance at the show. But of course, Rusty didn't know that.

# - Seventeen -

## Decision Time

Blakefield's Bank Holiday trophy show on the last day of August was held, as usual, at the Pony Club field at Watch Hill. It was an annual part of their calendar, designed to promote good all-round performance. It was also a useful practice for the Member's Cup competition held in September where there were cups and trophies to be won for every discipline, including a written test, with an overall champion in the different age groups. The prizes were all awarded at a big Christmas presentation party.

Unlike Member's Cup, where riders could win trophies in all of the different events, at the trophy show, only the overall winner of each age group was awarded. Riders earned points for their placing in equitation, handy pony, games and jumping. Amber would be competing in the twelve to fourteen-year-old age group, along with Emily, who would move up into the senior fifteen plus age group next year.

Although Rusty still looked under nourished with his pointy hips and narrow neck, he'd scrubbed up well following a bath. His coat shone like rare pink topaz, his black tail was silky and lustrous, and Amber had spaced his mane plaits out evenly in an attempt to disguise his thin neck. His tack gleamed, and the white numnah he wore was so clean, it seemed to shine. Amber wouldn't have said she felt proud of him, looking him over before she mounted for the first event, but at least he wasn't an embarrassment.

As she rode into the equitation ring for the first event, Amber looked around at her competitors. There was no sign of JoJo or Chelsea, who were both getting used to their new horses, and Amber wondered if they'd bother with Pony Club shows anymore now that they had their sights set on the sports of tetrathlon and eventing. She could see Emily just ahead of her on Pink. The pony's neck was arched magnificently as always, as if she loved to show off her impressive Mohican mane. She was such a stunning mare and stood out from the other ponies walking around the ring. Emily spotted her and waved, grinning with appreciation at the sight of Rusty, who apart from the absence of a mohawk, was almost identical to her own pony.

Amber waved back and joined the circling ponies, slotting in behind a red-haired girl riding a dark bay that she didn't recognise. This show always attracted riders from other clubs as well as Blakefield members and was well attended.

Amber counted six riders in her class. As well as herself and Emily, there was the red-haired girl she didn't know, two boys from her club: Ashley on his blue-eyed piebald pony, Bandit, and Jake on his chestnut, Ollie, and another girl she didn't know on a small grey.

Concentrating on Rusty's walk, she had to pull him out of the circling riders and join back in where there was a gap behind Emily. Rusty was walking so purposefully, he was getting too close to the grey pony in front of him. Emily half turned her head and gave Amber a wink of acknowledgement before the judge asked them to trot on. Amber steadied Rusty and lightly half halted him to keep him in check and at a respectful distance from Pink. Rusty obliged and took the contact quietly. Soon they were cantering, and Amber smiled as she rocked gently around the circle. Rusty had responded to the tiniest aid, struck off on the right leg and was cantering beautifully.

After watching the riders as a group, the judge asked them to line-up so that she could watch them perform individually. She did a double-take and chuckled when she noticed Pink and Rusty standing side by side, like twins.

Emily did her show first. She rode well, though Pink was pretty over-bent most of the time, showing her teeth as she curled up her top lip in an Elvis impression. The pony didn't enjoy working in controlled circles, much preferring charging about, and liked to show her objection whenever she was asked to do something she disapproved of.

Rusty did a beautiful show. He was so responsive but also obedient – their bond almost telepathic. As soon as Amber thought about asking him to do something, he did it without her even realising she'd given him the aid. It made her wonder about his past and how he'd ended up as a neglect case. Someone had obviously invested a great deal of time in him at some point as he was the best-schooled horse she'd ever ridden. As she pulled back into the line after saluting the judge, she marvelled at how quickly they'd become a team. She patted him in thanks. After all the problems with Molly, Rusty had quickly given her so much confidence in her riding. The way he went for her proved that she *could* ride and that her issues with Molly clearly hadn't been all her fault. Amber relaxed in the saddle as she settled to watch the remaining four riders.

As the sixth rider, Ashley, pulled out of the line for his turn, Amber noticed that he wasn't the last to go. Another horse was still waiting in line after him.

"Psst," Amber whispered to Emily. "There's seven in our class. I didn't see that one on the end. Who is it, do you know?"

Emily leaned forward to take a look, but the rider had her head turned away, watching Ashley's show. All they could see was dark hair in a hairnet. Emily shrugged. As they looked at the girl, Ashley changed rein, and the girl's head moved to face them. Amber and Emily recoiled simultaneously as they recognised the face. It was Elisha Templeton.

As Ashley pulled the moustachioed Bandit back into line, Elisha gracefully pulled out. She rode a pony-horse the colour of caramel. Amber wasn't sure if he was a large pony or a small horse – he looked about the same size as Rusty. Amber narrowed her eyes as she watched Elisha perform her show on the little horse. He looked familiar: plain, with no white markings, but clearly a quality, well-bred animal. His confirmation and movement were perfect. She knew she'd seen him somewhere before, but where?

Amber turned to look at her friend and raised her eyebrows. Emily understood the question and shook her head. She didn't know either.

Once Elisha was back in line, the judge set the riders off to walk around her in a circle again while she took a last look at them and decided on the placings. Amber couldn't see Elisha as she was behind her, but as she walked around, looking at Pink's quarters and her swishing black tail, it came to her.

"What's wrong with you?" Emily asked Amber as they rode away from the equitation, Amber sporting a blue second place rosette and Emily a green for fourth place. "You can't blame the judge for putting Elisha first. You and Rusty were brill, but I hate to say it, so was she.

That horse she's on is lovely. You've still got plenty of chances to beat her in the other events."

"That horse she's on is Darcy," Amber revealed through clenched teeth. "He's the horse I was meant to be getting on loan until his owner changed her mind and decided she didn't want him being ridden by a kid. Elisha's only a year older than me. She's hardly an adult, so how come *she's* got him?"

Amber wasn't only put out that Elisha was riding the horse she'd thought was going to be hers. When they'd been stood side by side in the line-up, being presented with their rosettes, Elisha had slid her eyes over Rusty and gave her customary smirk. When their eyes met, Amber had read her expression of triumph. Her foe looked like the cat who'd got the cream. Amber was certain that Elisha would know that she'd almost got Darcy, and that she'd be revelling in the knowledge that Amber hadn't been deemed worthy of him. And now, here she was with the prize, in more ways than one.

"Okay, boy," Amber whispered in Rusty's ear as she untacked him while they waited for the show jumping to begin. "You and I have to beat that witch face, do you hear? Can you do that for me?" She patted him tenderly, but Rusty had now been reunited with his haynet and didn't want to be fussed over. Laying his ears back, he shook his head at her. Clearly, he had no interest in her rivalry with Elisha Templeton. If Amber wanted to beat her opponent, it would be down to her.

***

"I assume it'll be okay for me to phone Yvonne when we get home to tell her not to expect Rusty back?" Mr Anderson asked later on as they walked away from the presentation of prizes with Amber clutching her first-ever trophy. It was, in fact, a beautiful red mahogany shield. There was a delicate painting of the outline of a horse's head in the centre with a series of silver plaques around the outside, showing the previous winners of the trophy. The names dated back to 2015. There were four blank plaques left, and her name would be getting engraved into one of them. She could keep the trophy for twelve months, then she'd have to bring it back to next year's show.

"Er…*yes*, I think so," she said, still staring at her prize in disbelief, taking in what had happened and what it meant. Her eyes scanned over some of the names of the previous winners: Deep Destiny, Lucetta, Disco Dazzler,

Indigo Star and Sky Pirate. "We just entered him today as 'Rusty', but he can't have that put on the trophy. I'll need to think of a good show name for him… for our future events and to go on this trophy." Amber smiled as she imagined winners in years to come holding the trophy and poring over the horses' names like she was. It had to be something that suited him. Something worthy of the star he was.

"Yes, you do that. And something else you can do, now that you've decided he's staying, is apologise to Caroline. Because of her, you've got a brilliant horse, but you've been ignoring her ever since he arrived. I think you need to thank her and apologise for your rudeness," Mrs Anderson pointed out, spoiling Amber's feeling of triumph by bringing Caroline up and reminding Amber of her ungrateful behaviour. She knew her mother was right, and she felt her ears redden as she briefly acknowledged how she had indeed been giving Caroline the cold shoulder since she'd been responsible for bringing Rusty home rather than Fox. Now that Caroline had been proved right, Amber was ashamed of her behaviour. But now wasn't the time to let that bring her down. This was meant to be one of the happiest moments of her life.

"Pow, pow!" Emily appeared, miming shooting Amber with a gun in each hand. She blew off the smoke from her imaginary weapons and declared, "Well done, Ammo. You let her have it with both barrels today. Did you see her face when the results were read out? You only beat her by a point. I thought she was going to explode!"

"I know. I can't believe I managed to beat Elisha on my little Rustbucket," Amber said, surprising herself with the affectionate nickname.

"He's no rust bucket. He may be a little rusty in that he's been out of practice for a while, but he knows what he's doing! He may be fifteen hands, but he's a proper Pony Club pony. He was amazing in the games. You won every race!"

"I know, and he was good in the handy pony too. It was my fault we didn't do very well in that – I couldn't get the horse shoes in the bucket as I couldn't see properly without my glasses. I really thought it had cost me the trophy."

"Yeah." Emily took the shield from Amber to admire it. "But luckily Ashley won that, not Elisha. Then you won the 75cm show jumping and Elisha won the 85cm, so you both got the same points for that event, since they use your best place in the jumping, and she'd already won the equitation. You *had* to win the games… and you did!"

"And you came second, helping to keep a point off Elisha. You're the reason I won. And well done for winning the 95cm jumping too. Pink was on fire in the jump-off." Amber congratulated her friend. Emily had come third overall. Pink had been fantastic in the jumping and games, but was too impatient for the handy pony and had several time fault penalties added for failing to complete some of the obstacles to the judge's satisfaction.

"Poop!" Emily replied. "You won because you and Rusty were good at everything. I bet you'll clear up at Member's Cup. I'm SOOOO pleased you beat Miss Snooty Pants. Did you hear what she said about Rusty and Pink after the equitation?"

"No, what did she say?

"I heard her say to that woman – Anita? The owner of the horse she's on today, that we were pathetic both having pink ponies like little girls wanting to be matchy-matchy. She said that Pink belonged in the circus and Rusty should have a career as a hat rack."

Amber bristled at the insult. She knew that it referred to her horse's ribby appearance. "Rusty gets *loads* of feed. He's been vetted, and there's nothing wrong with him. He's just a naturally slim build!" she protested. "Why does she have to be so horrible? I've no idea how she got the ride on Darcy. I wish she'd bog off back to the BS circuit and leave us in peace."

Amber had a lot to reflect on that evening once Rusty had been taken home and turned out with the Fell ponies. Thoughts swirled through her head all night as she sat in front of the TV after a bath, watching the pictures but taking nothing in.

Amber hadn't wanted Rusty. She'd been adamant about it and behaved like a brat when he'd been brought for her instead of Fox. But now, after a phone call to Yvonne, he was hers. And she knew it was right; he was the right horse for her. Not only had she won overall champion at her first-ever show with him, she'd also achieved her life's ambition of properly beating Elisha Templeton at the same time. Emily had been brilliant – truly and one hundred per cent thrilled for her win, with no resentment at all that she'd beaten her. Amber wondered if her friend's relaxed manner related to Mr Pryde's absence. He'd been with her brother Harry at a cricket event, so there'd been no stress. Mrs Pryde watched her daughter quietly and offered congratulations whatever her placing, whereas Emily's dad was only ever happy with first place.

Amber considered how lucky she was. Rusty hadn't been her choice, but deep down, she'd known that she preferred him to Fox. She'd let her perception of other people's expectations and attitudes cloud her judgement, but Amber had been wrong and should have known better than to judge Rusty based on his appearance, thinking that everyone else would too. But everyone loved Rusty. It was like fate had intervened and made sure Rusty came to her even when she couldn't see for herself that it was meant to be. She knew what it was like to be judged by appearance – it happened to her all the time, and people's judgements weren't usually positive. She hated it, yet she'd done the same thing.

Hearing that Elisha had called him a hat rack made her protective instinct flare inside of her. *How dare she?*

*She was only saying what you were thinking.* The voice in her head pointed out.

*I know*. Amber berated herself for still being influenced by concern over other people's opinions. *When am I going to learn to think for myself?*

*You did today.* The voice reminded her. *You made the choice to keep Rusty.*

*I'm not sure it was a choice,* Amber mused. *I think it was written in the stars.*

# - Eighteen -

# Stolen Thunder

Summer merged into autumn, and Amber returned to school. She was now in Year 9, but nothing had changed. She'd get to choose her options for Year 10 next spring and would be able to drop some subjects, but sadly there'd be no option to kiss goodbye to her least favourites: maths and physics, as they were compulsory.

During September, Amber continued to ride after school while it was still light enough. But as the leaves shrivelled and fell from the trees and the landscape's palette muted, the days shortened with the suggestion of winter.

With mounted rallies and games practices coming to an end, Mr Clark, the games coach, had come up with the idea of organising an end-of-year indoor games competition for local clubs. It was just for some festive fun, but he figured it would also help him to choose the team members for next year's Area Games. He'd named it 'The Blakefield Blitz', but as the competition was to be held in December, the kids had soon rechristened it 'The Blakefield Blitzen.'

Matthew was desperate to be chosen for a team, but as he would be eleven in December, he was out of juniors and so would have to compete as a senior if selected. Competition for places would be fierce. JoJo wasn't interested in a place on the Area Games team as it was held around the same time as the Junior International Tetrathlon competition, and she was determined to be selected for the Northern England team. But she was happy to take part in the senior 'Blitzen' competition.

Amber too, was looking forward to it as Rusty continued to excel at games. As the evening light grew shorter and curtailed hacks in the forestry, most of Amber's after school riding consisted of games practices in the Jones' paddock. The three of them occasionally used one lane to work on their hand overs, but more often they had three lanes to race each other. JoJo continued to win most of the time, but not always. In races that didn't require remounting, where Amber was at a disadvantage due to her inability to vault on, she sometimes managed to beat her friend. JoJo seemed to appreciate having some serious competition and would happily high five Amber when she triumphed. Although it was just the three of them racing in fading light in JoJo's paddock, Amber felt an unbelievable sense of victory. She'd never thought she had a chance of beating JoJo in anything. Ever.

"The Blitzen will be fab," she gushed at the end of one session on a Wednesday evening. "With us three and Emily on a team, we'll be a force!"

"Oh…er…I didn't realise you were thinking of a place on the team," JoJo said, her face unusually tense.

"Why? Don't you think I'm good enough?"

"What? Of course you're *good enough.* Duh, you're brilliant. But they won't let you ride Rusty in the team. They'll be sticking to the Pony Club rules, and Rusty is over height. You can only ride ponies. They have to be a maximum of 14.2hh for the official team competitions."

So that was that. Rusty was ruled out for being too big. It seemed ironic after her worries that he was too small. She'd been so keen to be a part of the competition, she couldn't bear the thought of missing out. Honey was brought out to see if she could save the day, as she'd done before in the past, but it was no good. She was too slow and too spooky. She might jump water trays and fillers without hesitation, but she wasn't keen on flags, bottles, or mugs on poles. JoJo tried to be encouraging.

"Maybe with a bit more practice, she'll get used to the flags and everything. And, you know, she's steady and accurate…"

"It's no good. Mr Clark won't pick me with her to be on the same team with you lot. If there are enough people to make up two senior teams, you'll be the A-team. I want to be with you and Emily, not on a B team. I'm sure Ashley and Jake will want to do it, and some others. I definitely won't make it on to your team with Honeybun."

"Aww, bummer," JoJo commiserated. "What can we do?"

***

As September came to an end, the club's Member's Cup competition was held on the last Sunday. The written test had been completed under strict test conditions at Mrs Best's house on the Friday evening, with all members being given an allocated time to turn up and do their test. Amber had revised all week by reading her Manual of Horsemanship from cover to cover and highlighting key facts she knew she'd struggle to remember, such as a horse's body temperature at rest, heart and respiration rate.

On the night, her revision paid off, and she felt she'd done well, but the results weren't to be revealed until Sunday. Results and rosettes would be given out on the day, but winners would have to wait for the Christmas presentation evening to receive their trophies.

The day couldn't have gone better for Amber. She didn't expect to win anything, mainly because JoJo was in her age group, but somehow, she managed to top her in the equitation, jumping and games, which she won thanks to the third and final game being 'walk, trot and lead'. When the start flag dropped, riders had to walk to the top pole, then trot back to, and around the first pole and continue in trot back up to the top pole. Most ponies couldn't contain their excitement in this race. So used to galloping away from the start line when the flag fell, most of them attempted to jog in the walk leg. If Mr Clark spotted anyone jogging – which was everyone except

Amber – he shouted at them to turn a circle. By the time Rusty strode to the top pole, he was already well in the lead. The same continued in the trot phase, with most of the ponies breaking into canter and being penalised with more circles. Rusty didn't break from walk or trot once. When Amber reached the top pole for the second time, she flung herself off, ready to tow Rusty to the finish by leading him as she ran ahead of him. Rusty needed no dragging, however, and it was Amber who had to run as fast as she could in jodhpur boots to keep up with her horse as he cantered to the finish. She was the one being dragged. They completed the race miles ahead of the others, Amber gasping, "woah boy! We're finished!"

"He'd be a great games pony, if he were a pony," Mr Clark commented, shaking his head.

"Yes, about that," Amber said, recovering her breath. "Is there any way I could take part in the Blakefield Blitz on him? I'd love to do it, and I know Rusty would too."

"Sorry Amber…" Mr Clark paused as he recorded the results of the race. "No can do. It's a Pony Club team competition, so we have to stick to the rules. Your wee man there is over height, so I'm afraid not."

Amber's disappointment about the Blitz was momentarily forgotten when the riders assembled at the end of the day to find out the results. Emily had won the jumping, Ashley got the handy pony, JoJo was the best turned out, Elisha won the equitation riding Darcy again, and to her utter amazement, Amber had won the games and the written test. With her good performances in all of the other sections, it made her the overall champion… again! She couldn't believe it. In two outings with Rusty, she'd won four trophies with him. She'd dreamed of collecting a horde of silverware when she got Molly-the-proven-competition-pony, but it hadn't happened. Now here she was with her 'hat rack' rescue horse cleaning up. She'd triumphed over Elisha again and even managed to trump JoJo. It was like something from one of her wildest day dreams. Rusty was just the best.

"You've done it again, champ," Emily said, jumping on Amber and hugging her. "I managed to get a trophy in the jumping to keep Dad happy, and JoJo is the top-prettiest-ponce, so we've all won something."

"Oy!" JoJo protested. "I deserve that trophy. I had to clean all Matty's tack and plait up Flash for him too cos he's useless. He didn't get best turned out though – he hadn't cleaned his boots!"

"Speaking of boys," Amber said, turning to Emily. "Where's Harry? I thought he'd be doing this on Fudgey?"

"Mmm, he hasn't had much time for riding recently. My dad's got him doing loads of cricket and football. He's on school and town teams for both." Emily suddenly slumped, and her bouncy, happy attitude vanished. "If he doesn't ride, I can see Dad deciding that Fudge is surplus to requirements." Tears welled in her eyes.

"Do you mean you think he'd sell him?" Amber asked, reaching out a hand and placing it on Emily's shoulder. Emily nodded.

"Everything's a bit crap at home at the moment, to be honest. Well, it has been for a while really." She lowered herself onto the ramp of Amber's trailer, and the other girls sat on either side of her, concerned. Emily was like a different person. She seemed to have shrunk.

"Mum and Dad keep arguing and falling out. Mainly about Harry. He's sporty like Dad but not doing very well at school. I try to help him with his reading and homework, but he struggles. Mum wants him to do less sport and get a tutor to help him with schoolwork, but Dad doesn't agree. He says Harry doesn't need it and should concentrate on sport as he's good at it and could have a great future as a professional sportsman. He doesn't need school," she let out a big, pent up sigh. "And of course, he wants me to be more competitive and do more with Pink, but I'm not bothered. I'm happy doing local shows. Plus, he's always taking Harry here, there and everywhere, so Mum would have to run me all over the country if I started doing British Show jumping. She hasn't time for that, on top of work and everything. She's always telling Dad to back off and leave me alone," her voice started to thicken. "He…he says I've got no ambition. But I have…just not in a competitive sense. They're always rowing – I think they might be going to split up."

Amber was speechless. How had Emily been keeping this to herself? How had she been able to act so bubbly and happy with all of that going on? Not knowing what to say, she put her arms around Emily and hugged her. JoJo joined in and the three of them sat, wrapped in each other's arms. It was an unexpected ending to the day

Emily soon shook them off and wiped her eyes, reassembling her smile before she went back to her mum. "Thanks guys," she attempted a laugh. "And sorry for stealing your thunder, Amber. It should have been us congratulating you, not you two commiserating with me. You and Rusty were fan-dabby-dozy today."

"All for one and one for all," Amber replied, quoting their tetrathlon team motto.

***

"That was a shocker," JoJo said as they watched Emily walk away from them, lacking her earlier bounce.

"You're telling me. We need to do something to cheer her up. Something involving Chelsea too. We haven't seen her for ages. We need to do something together."

"Yes, good idea. What do you suggest?" JoJo looked expectantly at Amber.

"Leave it with me," Amber said. "I think I have a plan."

# - Nineteen -

## A Game of Horses

"You've done WHAT?" JoJo replied, giving Amber a feeling of déjà vu. It wasn't long since JoJo had said those very words when she'd discovered Amber had broken her collarbone and nearly put herself out of the postal shoot. But this time, it was good news she was delivering. Or at least she thought so.

It was two weeks later, and October half-term was another two weeks away. Amber and JoJo were making the most of a cold but sunny Sunday to take Pluto for a ride in the forestry with Rusty. Mrs Anderson was also with them, acting as a chaperone for the young horse, and to keep an eye on Georgia on Pearl, but they rode well back from the girls, allowing them to talk in private.

"Come on, Plute," JoJo urged the gelding to step up his pace in order to keep up with Rusty's march. The young horse towered over Rusty, but his long legs still couldn't keep up with the smaller horse beside him. Responding to his rider's aids, he picked up the speed slightly only to have Rusty jab his head out at him, ears back in warning. Even in walk, Rusty was competitive and guarded his place at the front. He wasn't going to let anyone overtake him without a fight.

"So, you've asked Mrs Best and Mr Clark if you can organise a separate horse section of the Blakefield Blitz, and they've agreed?" For some reason, her voice sounded incredulous.

"Yes. What's wrong with that?" She didn't pause to let JoJo answer. "I got the idea from Rusty – he's a horse and good at games, so there must be others who are too. Did you know there's even a Mounted Games Association? They allow horses up to 15hh to be used, and riders can be any age, so why shouldn't we have a horses' team? Games doesn't just have to be for ponies. And even if they're not any good, it doesn't matter. It's just for fun. And for charity. Mr Clark said I'd need to get at least two other teams to do it, and if I can, we're going to turn the horse part into a charity event. We'll donate their entry fee, plus I thought I'd run some stalls and things while the ponies are competing in their part, as I won't be doing that. The horses' event will follow on after the ponies. There's no upper or lower age limit for riders, so long as they're on a horse, not a pony. It could even be parents making up teams, or older club members."

"Er… you say you need to get at least two *other* horse teams for it to go ahead…that makes it sound like you've already got one sorted?" JoJo looked down at Amber in disbelief. Who was this girl, organising teams, turning them into charity events? This wasn't the Amber she knew.

Amber cocked her head and smiled up at JoJo. "We're the team. Us four musketeers." She laughed at the look of confusion on her friend's face. "There'll be me on Rusty, obvs, and you and Chelsea on your new horses and then Emily."

"WHAT?" JoJo almost yelled. She threw a glance over her shoulder to check that she hadn't got Mrs Anderson's attention.

"Everything okay there?" Amber's mum called from behind them, mounted on Honey, riding alongside Georgia on Pearl.

"Yes, fine, thanks," JoJo called back before turning to Amber once again and whispering furiously. "Pluto can't do a games competition. He's so long and lanky, he'll probably tie his own legs in a knot and fall over. Plus, I don't think he can move fast enough." She gave him another kick to ask him to keep up. "He was really forward going over jumps when I tried him, but he's been a bit chilled since we brought him home. I don't think he's got much of a racing instinct. And Chelsea has gone all serious-eventer now and won't want her dressage pupil charging up and down bending poles in case it blows his mind. And Emily? Amber, are you forgetting something? Emily doesn't have a horse!"

"I've sorted that," Amber said mysteriously. "I've got a horse arranged for Emily to borrow. And Pluto will be fine. It'll probably be good for him, in fact. I read online that the show jumper, Shay Scott, does some games with her young jumpers. She said it's good to give them something else to think about, and it gets them to use different parts of their bodies, so it reduces repetitive strain from the same type of work all the time. She also said she trains her show jumpers in bending poles as it sharpens them up and helps them learn to take turns at speed in a jump-off. I know that doesn't concern you and Chelsea as neither of you will need to do jump offs, but if you can teach your horses to stay balanced coming out of a turn, it means you can take strides out at speed, and that's something you both do need. Plus, games helps you improve your balance and coordination, and you have to use your body weight to influence the horse. What's not to love about that for two cross-country horses?"

"Wow, you've done your homework," JoJo said, clearly impressed, her ears pricking at the mention of the new rising star on the international show jumping circuit, Shay Scott. "And I can see the argument, but Chelsea will never go for it. She's super serious about the eventing now and won't take time out to do a games competition, even if it is for charity.

"I need you to help me convince her. You're in the same boat, with a young horse so you can persuade her that it'll be good for their education. Plus, I agree, Chelsea *has* got super serious. She'd driven and focussed and knows what she wants, but she needs to have some fun too. I think we need to gently remind her of that. Chelsea will be training away all alone, but the whole point of this is doing something together, being a team again, looking out for each other, and giving Emily something good to focus on. We can't say 'all for one and one for all' and not mean it. So, what do you say, are you in? Will you do it? Will you help me?"

"I say, I don't know who you are or what you've done with the real Amber, but yes, I'll give it a try. If I'm allowed," she added. "Pluto was pretty expensive, and I'm not sure Mum and Dad will be too keen on me using my future cross-country specialist for games, but you know me, I'll work on them and get them to agree. Oh, and by the way – if we're doing this, we're not just doing it for fun. We'll be in it to win it."

"Great!" Amber gave a little jump in the saddle that made Rusty flick his ears back in irritation, as if he was telling her to sit still. "So, shall we message Chelsea tonight and get her onside? If we can get her to agree to it, then we can tell Emily. And it's not like it's happening next week. We'll have two months to practise!"

"Oh yeah, a horse for Emily? You've managed to 'borrow' a horse for her? Do tell."

***

As JoJo predicted, her parents were not thrilled with the idea of their new star horse being used for games. But of course, JoJo was not to be deterred and worked her persuasive magic on them. This was helped along by subjecting them to a stream of Shay Scott training videos on YouTube which showed her 'playing games' with her top show jumpers. Eventually won over by seeing the way Shay was able to increase and decrease her mounts' speed, turn them on a sixpence, and maintain their balance, without ever hauling on their mouths or being rough with them in any way, they decided it was worth a try. So long as JoJo was patient with Pluto and took her time to build up to actually racing.

"We have lift off!" she announced to Amber. "Let's begin Operation Convince Chelsea."

Just as they feared, Chelsea was completely uninterested in Amber's quest to reunite the girls in another team event. "I loved being on the tetrathlon team with you all; you know I did. It was fantastic, but I can't do games. Harris is at a delicate stage in his training, and I'm trying to improve his collection. Bombing up and down bending poles is never going to help him develop as an eventer. I'm sorry, but no, I can't do it."

Resistance is futile, JoJo private messaged Amber, before challenging her to a bet as to how long it would take to convince Chelsea to join them. Amber suggested the coming Saturday as a deadline. JoJo accepted with relish, stating that it would be well before then.

*Does JoJo ever not get her own way?* Amber wondered when Chelsea officially became a team member on Thursday evening, having also been practically brainwashed by JoJo's onslaught of Shay Scott videos.

It's brilliant, Chelsea gushed, doing a complete 180 on her original view. How agile and responsive she gets her horses by doing games with them. And you can see they love it too. It'll be great to add it into Harris' training program over the winter.

Mmm hmm, JoJo messaged back. I hate to say I told you so.

Well, Amber, you've got your wish. You've made a team of three, but four horsemen of the apocalypse are needed. So come on, tell us about this horse you've got for Emily. Whose is it? Chelsea pressed

Amber had enjoyed her little secret while it lasted. It was a pleasant and unusual feeling to be the one who knew something that others didn't but wanted to. But it was time. She had to tell them what she'd been up to.

# - Twenty -

## The Blitzen

The day of the Blakefield Blitzen was dull and drizzly, though that wouldn't matter as the event was indoors. Although the weather wasn't going to bother them, Amber was pleased that the day was mild as she was going to be running the stalls all morning until the horses' event in the afternoon. She'd be indoors, behind the viewing gallery, so it would be dry, but there was no heating, and it was December. Draughts would be wafting around like jet streams. She'd come prepared with several layers of clothes, a hat, gloves and scarf.

Amber watched her mother and Georgia erecting the folding tables they'd brought for their stalls and shivered. But not because of the cold. This was going to be a big event. The main part of it, organised by Mr Clark and Mrs Best; mounted games for junior and senior teams, had attracted entries from all over the county as well as from the North East and Scotland. Lured by the chance to perform for their club's selectors in the hopes of being chosen for next year's Area Games teams, riders were also looking forward to some festive fun. All of the Blakefield team ponies – and horses – would be festooned in red tinsel to match the riders' red sweatshirts. But the rest of the day was all down to Amber. The team event for horses in the afternoon was her brainchild, as was the idea to run a range of stalls throughout the day to aid the Brooke charity. It would all be featured in the local newspaper, and a crew from the TV news might possibly attend too.

Amber couldn't believe that her idea, centred partly around Emily and reuniting the tetrathlon team, and partly around her desire to compete on Rusty in something he was so good at, but was excluded from, had been accepted and was going ahead. Four other horse teams had entered, so her charity event was also going to be a proper competition. She tingled in anticipation. After all their preparation for today's event, it was finally here.

Amber helped Georgia cover the tables in orange tablecloths. The colour had been chosen to match the Brooke's logo. Her mind floated back to the memory of the day the team was re-formed. Since she'd got JoJo and Chelsea onside, she'd been able to break the news to Emily about her idea and let her know how she could be involved. She smiled to herself as she replayed it.

You're kidding? Emily had messaged when she'd revealed the identity of the secret horse she'd arranged for her friend to ride in the team. Lady? The thoroughbred Caroline is turning into an event horse? She's going to let a stranger borrow her eventer-in-training to charge about doing Pony Club Games?

Yep, she'd typed back, loving the feeling of being able to surprise everyone with her plan. Judging by the range of shocked emojis that popped up from all of them, none of the girls had guessed that Emily's mount would be Lady.

How'd you manage that? I thought you weren't speaking to her.

Amber paused before she typed back. A shawl of shame draped itself around her making her skin itch and prickle as she remembered how she'd treated Caroline after Rusty's arrival. She'd blamed Caroline for bringing him to her, rather than Fox, even though she'd known, deep down somewhere almost bottomless, that the chestnut gelding wasn't right for her.

It was always difficult to apologise, and she'd squirmed inside on the day when she'd popped into Lady's stable to make her peace with Caroline. Caroline kept sweeping as Amber fumbled over her words, but she knew it wasn't out of rudeness. She felt as uncomfortable as Amber did and didn't want to make it worse for the girl by stopping and staring at her as she revealed the reasons for her ungrateful behaviour and sought to make up for it. Never looking at Amber, Caroline mumbled, "It's okay," and "I understand."

Hoping that she meant it, Amber ploughed on, filling Caroline in on how'd she'd been doing with Rusty, his unexpected skill at mounted games and her idea for the charity horse teams at the Blakefield Blitz.

"Wow. That sounds amazing. Good for you," Caroline's eyes flicked up to Amber as she scooped dirty straw into the wheelbarrow that stood between them.

"Thanks… yeah…er…but we have a bit of a problem…We'd really like to reunite our tetrathlon team from the summer for it: me, JoJo, Chelsea and Emily. JoJo and Chelsea both have horses now, but Emily doesn't. She can't be on the team on her pony, Pink, as the whole point is that it's a separate competition for horses, so…"

"She could borrow this one," Caroline leaned her mucking out tools against the wall and gave Lady's neck a rub. It was like she'd read Amber's mind. She'd just been working up to proposing that very idea but was worried Caroline would think she'd only apologised so she could beg a favour. And here she was, offering without even needing to be asked. She was such an amazing person, Amber's eyes swam.

"What, *really*? You wouldn't mind?"

"Not at all. Well, your friend can try her and see how she reacts to it, see if she's suitable, but she's been pretty laid back with everything I've done with her so I don't think there'll be any problem. She's not doing much at the moment, and she's probably a bit bored, so it'll be good for her." Caroline focussed on smoothing Lady's mane to avoid meeting Amber's gaze as the girl stood, staring at her. It was looking rather wintery and shaggy at the moment and would need to be pulled if she was going to be seen in public

"Well, I'll, er, tell her, and the others, and we'll see if we can arrange something," Amber said, still unable to take her eyes off Caroline.

"Yeah, and maybe you should invite her up here one weekend to go for a hack out with you, on Lady. Probably best if she meets her and rides her first, gets a feel for her before you start introducing her to games. And in the meantime, I'll start getting her used to neck reining when I'm riding her out.

"You are unbelievable. In a good way! Do you want to be our team trainer?"

And that's what had happened. During half-term, the girls had all met for a hack in the foresty; Chelsea boxing Harris through to the farm and the Andersons picking Emily up so that she could ride Lady. Amber had worried a bit about how the four horses might get on together: two youngsters, an ex-racehorse and the pint-sized Rusty who thought he was Seabiscuit. The last time the girls had all ridden together in the forest, during a treasure hunt, the ponies had gotten themselves wildly overexcited. Amber didn't want the same to happen with the horses. As it was all her idea, she felt responsible for everyone and hoped the horses would remain calm. Amber had a dread of them all starting to race each other, and it ending in disaster like the ride with JoJo and Elisha had when the girls had lost control of their racing ponies.

But she needn't have worried. Rusty took the lead, as usual, but was easily matched by Lady, who strode along beside him, her large ears flopping, totally ignoring his angry protestations that she was in his space. Amber and Emily laughed at Lady's aloofness as Rusty repeatedly threatened her, and she continued to act as if he didn't exist. They had a couple of tentative canters, worried about explosive bucks or bolts, but nothing happened. Lady immediately went to the front as she was effortlessly fast. Rusty put his head down and battled to keep up with her, though again, she had no interest in him. Pluto and Harris were happy to lollop along behind them, but when they pulled up, the young horses looked bright-eyed and had a spring in their step.

“Good boy,” JoJo patted Pluto, whose veins were standing up under his clipped coat. “That’s perked you up a bit, hasn’t it?”

It was too dark to practise games after school and too wet to use Caroline or JoJo’s paddock at weekends, and so a large arena with floodlights was hired near Chelsea’s place every Wednesday and Saturday evening for them to start introducing the three novice horses to the sport of mounted games. Although the Andersons had bought a bigger, horse-sized trailer, Caroline always offered to transport Lady and Rusty to the arena and, as she was there anyway, she became the team’s unofficial trainer.

They’d started slowly. First, they’d used jump wings placed in a line to teach the horses to bend around them.

This had begun in walk, before progressing to trotting and slow cantering. Caroline helped them to teach the horses to respond to their changes of position and to neck reining. Once all of the horses could bend in canter up and down a line of ‘bending wings’, they’d worked on handing over a baton, using a whip as their baton. It quickly became apparent that Rusty would need to go either first or last in the bending race since he threatened to bite any horse who approached him.

As the competition approached, the Jones' homemade equipment was brought through so the team could practise the other games they'd be doing at the Blitzen: mug, bottle and five flag. Amber had discussed with Mr Clark that none of their games should involve having to mount and dismount, due to the difficulty for some riders to remount large horses that they couldn't vault on to. She'd also convinced him to have Rusty's favourite game: walk, trot and lead, as their final game. It wasn't an official Pony Club game, but Mr Clark agreed that it would be a fun finale to see the riders racing each other on foot with their horses in tow.

All went well with the training except that Lady took an unexpected exception to the flags when the flag race was introduced and wouldn't go near them. Emily tried her best but Lady wasn't going to be persuaded.

"What are we going to do?" Emily panicked. There's only the four of us, so we all have to do every race.

Caroline promised to work on de-sensitising Lady to the flags in time for the competition, but as the day of the event got closer, the mare continued to object to them. The team were starting to get anxious as, without a fifth member, all horses had to do all of the races. But with just over a week to go before the event, the Andersons received a phone call.

Mr Anderson took the call. There were lots of 'mmm's' and 'I see' and 'of course', but Amber frowned, wondering why her dad kept shooting her worried glances. When the call ended, he turned to his daughter, bracing himself for the reaction he knew was coming his way.

"That was Mrs Best. I think we've got a solution to your problem with Lady and the flags," he said, hopefully.

"What?" Amber was suspicious.

"She's er, got another member who's heard about your horsey games team and wants to join in. So you'll have a fifth member. She'll be able to do the flag race!"

Amber looked at him, raising her eyebrows in a question. "So…? Who is it?"

"It's…er…Elisha. Elisha Templeton."

"You WHAT? Elisha? How? She doesn't even have a horse anymore. How can she do it?"

"Well…Mrs B says she's going to be riding… Darcy."

"DARCY? The horse Anita wouldn't let me have on loan because she didn't want him *being charged around on by some kid?* Does she know what mounted games is?"

"Yes, I know. Reading between the lines, I think Anita has heard that the TV news are likely to be doing a piece on the event, and she'd like to be involved. She's offered a very generous donation to the charity."

"Oh, I see! So she's bought Elisha's place on the team, knowing it would be an absolute no otherwise."

Mrs Anderson joined in. "I know you don't like her Amber, and it's a shock that Anita is letting her use Darcy, but she can't be excluded. You need a fifth member, really, and part of the reason why you've done all of this is because Emily's having family problems. Elisha's having family problems too – her dad's left, her brother is getting himself into all sorts of trouble, we've heard, and she's lost her horses too. Poor girl. Be the better person and give her a chance. You know how good it's been for you having the girls as friends; maybe that's what Elisha needs right now – some friends."

Amber rolled her eyes and resisted the temptation to stamp her foot like an angry sheep. Instead, she stomped upstairs to message her friends and impart the bad news.

***

"Do you want these here?" Georgia asked, interrupting her thoughts. Amber snapped back into the present and saw that Georgia was referring to the boards that she'd pinned information and pictures about the Brooke onto. She'd done a school project on the charity last year and spent ages mounting it all onto coloured card. She was pleased she'd kept it as it now made a perfect display to showcase the charity to everyone who'd be attending.

"Yes, please, that's great." She smiled at Georgia, who'd jumped at the chance to come along and help out all day. Chelsea was also going to come and help with the stalls, as, like Amber, she wasn't riding until the afternoon. JoJo and Emily were both on the Blakefield senior team, on Merry and Pink, along with Matthew, Ashley and Jake. They'd said they'd help while the juniors were riding so they should be along some time soon.

Amber, Georgia and Mrs Anderson finished setting up the tables and arranging the stalls. They had a 'Pin the Tail on the Donkey', 'Guess the Name of the Hobby Horse', 'Throw Horseshoes in a Bucket' a raffle and a cake stall. Emily had assured her that she and her mum loved baking and would bring a range of cakes and tray bakes to sell. Amber hoped she'd bring enough. They were bound to sell like hot-cakes!

In the arena, Amber could see Mr Clark and Mrs Best with her husband and daughter setting up the poles and equipment for the juniors' first race. Despite the Elisha-spanner-in- the-works, she couldn't wait for her turn later on. They'd prove that games wasn't just for ponies. Horses could play too.

# - Twenty-One -

## At Last

Elisha was poised on the start line for the final race of the horses' competition. Amber's maths suggested that the Blakefield team were in the lead, but she didn't trust that she was right. She wasn't good at keeping track of numbers. Whatever the score, she knew they still needed to do their best in this race to ensure they were the overall winners.

It wasn't looking good. The final race was meant to be Chelsea, JoJo, Emily and Amber, but the girls had made the last-minute decision to substitute Elisha for Chelsea. Harris had been pretty spooked by all the noise and atmosphere of the event. It was nothing like what he'd experienced before, and Chelsea had to ride him slowly and carefully in his races to keep him calm. Chelsea was glad that she'd taken part and felt that it'd been good for Harris' education. But she also knew when enough was enough, and made the call to give her place in the last race to Elisha.

On the start line, waiting for the flag to fall, Darcy was pawing the ground, eager to move, just like the other horses waiting for the race to begin. After all the galloping about in the other races, Amber knew that the horses were expecting to tear away as soon as the flag dropped. But this was the walk, trot and lead. The horses had to start the race in walk. If they broke into trot or canter, they were penalised by having to ride a circle. Looking at how hyped up the horses were, Amber knew this race was going to be carnage. At least it would be an entertaining finale for the audience.

And, they were off. The starter's flag fell, and the first horses in each team leapt forward. Line stewards immediately signalled to every rider to circle. Amber gripped her reins tightly and held her breath in anticipation. She was the last rider to go for the Blakefield team, and this was Rusty's best race. But if they were too far behind by the time it came to their turn, would they be able to catch up?

Amber's breath escaped her like a punctured tyre as she stood in her stirrups to watch the progress of the race. Elisha had managed to settle Darcy, and he was now trotting back towards them at a good speed.

It was like watching a film. It didn't seem real that Elisha had become her teammate. When she'd found out that the girl was joining their team, Amber had felt crushed. She didn't want Elisha on their team. She wanted it to be just the four of them, like the tetrathlon. They all trusted each other, looked out for each other and never criticised or humiliated each other with the kind of slyly disguised but still nasty comments that Elisha was queen of. She'd feared that Elisha's presence would demoralise everyone and dim the lights of their sparkling team spirit.

But it hadn't turned out that way. If anything was lacking in their unity, Elisha wasn't to blame for it.

By the time it was announced that Elisha was joining the team, there was only one more practice before the competition she could attend. The girls had discussed, in advance, which races she might do. Emily and Amber were adamant that she was only doing the flag race, since Lady wouldn't go near the flags, but JoJo and Chelsea thought this was unfair.

There are five races. You can't have her come all the way to Highland Park just to do one race. She'll have to have two at least, Chelsea had objected when Amber messaged them all to fill them in.

No, she doesn't, Amber stropped, still narked that her marvellous idea was being spoiled by Elisha Templeton. She'll get what she's given. This is our team. She wasn't invited. Elisha can't expect to barge her way in and just get what she wants. We don't even know if Darcy will be any good. I bet she hasn't been practising with him.

You are being a bit mean, JoJo said. I bet she *will* have been practising. She likes to win; you know she does. And remember how you felt when we did that ride, and she wouldn't let you join us? You were really upset. Now you're doing the same to Elisha.

Yes, I do remember that. I remember how you did nothing to stop her and didn't stick up for me, Amber messaged back with lots of exclamation marks. So, I'd say this is karma. You reap what you sow.

JoJo didn't reply, and Amber suddenly worried that she'd upset her, but Chelsea typed back, Let's just see how practice goes. She can try all the races, and we'll decide who's doing what based on that.

At their one and only full team practice, Caroline had boxed Lady and Rusty to the arena as usual, giving Amber a lift too. Emily had met them there. She'd been dropped off to wait for them and had switched the floodlights on. As soon as Amber dropped down from the cab, Emily pounced on her, thrusting something soft into her hands.

"What's this?" Amber asked, unfolding the dark material to find it was a hooded fleece. In the centre was a red circle containing a black image of a snarling cat. Beneath the logo was the word 'Thundercats' in sharp, blood-red lettering. "What the -?"

"And I've got this one," Emily pointed to the fleece she was modelling. Also black, it bore an image of a white mouse and a bespectacled mole. "Danger Mouse!" she said, pointing to the words, in bright red and yellow. I thought these would be a good way to welcome our new team member. Put yours on."

“Oh, I…I don’t know…” Amber was dreading having to spend time with Elisha at their final practice, and she’d made some hard comments in her messages to the other girls. But this. She wasn’t comfortable with this. Elisha was on their team, whether she liked it or not. She couldn’t do this to her. It hadn’t been Elisha’s choice to have both of her lovely horses sold. For them to wear tops bearing their names seemed insensitive…cruel even. She was surprised at Emily for going to all the trouble of finding and ordering the tops, just to spite Elisha. It didn’t seem like her at all.

“Come on, Amber, don’t be a wimp. Elisha has been absolutely awful to both of us. She probably thinks she’s coming to be the queen bee of our team. She’ll be trying to take over and tell us what to do even though this is all down to you for organising it. Elisha won’t want you getting all the attention. She’ll have something horrible to say straight away. Just watch. She’s a bully, and she loves intimidating people. Remember what Chelsea said at the tetrathlon? She said bullies need squashing before they get going. So that’s what we’re doing: we’re just getting the first dig in to let her know we’re not scared of her.

We're standing up for ourselves and showing her we won't put up with anything, that's all."

Amber knew that everything Emily said was probably true, but she still felt her cheeks burn as she allowed her friend to talk her into putting the fleece on. The red logo on the front was so conspicuous, it felt like a target inviting someone to shoot at it.

As the girls mounted and started warming up in the arena, the heat in Amber's face blazed to match the Thundercat logo. Chelsea had noticed her and Emily's choice of clothing immediately. Amber was aware of her glaring eyes boring into her as she trotted Rusty around the arena and noticed her shaking her head. Soon Chelsea had joined JoJo, and the two of them rode around together, whispering.

Feeling utterly wretched, Amber headed towards the arena gate, intending to change back into the top she'd arrived in. But it was too late. Just as she started riding straight towards the gate, Elisha entered, mounted on Darcy. She looked like she'd been about to say something, but she stopped as soon as Amber pulled up in front of her. Her eyes quickly lowered as she took in Amber's outfit before rising again. She held Amber's gaze for a moment before turning Darcy and riding away. The look said everything.

*She knows,* Amber thought. *She knows exactly why I'm wearing this. Wait 'til she sees what Emily's got on.* Getting one over on the girl who'd plagued her thoughts for so long should have cheered her. But it didn't. At all. The look in Elisha's eyes made Amber ashamed. She'd have to make up for it by being nice to her. Emily wouldn't like it, but maybe she was taking her own family problems out on Elisha.

"Right girls, let's get started," Caroline called in her loudest whisper. As the riders headed towards her, ready to begin, Amber's mind whirled. Elisha was never going to be her friend, but maybe it was time they tried to get along. Right now, Amber was the one who had everything she wanted, while Elisha had nothing. Perhaps the power balance between them had shifted. Amber didn't feel the pressure to prove herself as much as she once had. She'd had success; she had friends. Maybe it was time to let go of her Elisha-grudge.

By the end of the practice, they'd agreed who would participate in each race. As the bending was an all-out speed race, and Harris was easily the slowest of the five, it was an easy decision to swap Chelsea for Elisha. JoJo was right – Elisha had been practising. Amber had no idea how she'd managed to persuade Anita to let her use Darcy for games, but he was pretty proficient. The same height as Rusty, he was a close match in skill. Pangs of jealousy threatened to sideline Amber's earlier resolution to forgive and forget.

The mug race would be Amber, JoJo, Emily and Chelsea. Elisha would take Emily's place in the bottle and five flag, and the final race – Amber's favourite - walk, trot and lead, would be Amber, JoJo, Emily and Chelsea.

"So that's it then, we're all ready for Sunday," Amber said after everyone had rugged and loaded their horses, ready to head home. She'd taken the Thundercat top off and replaced it with her own. "Good luck with the ponies," she directed at JoJo and Emily, who would also be competing in the senior event on Merry and Pink. "Hopefully the charity stalls and raffle will go well too, and we'll make a good bit to send to the Brooke."

"Yep, me and Mum will be doing lots of baking, so I'll bring them to the stalls as soon as we arrive." Emily was still wearing her Danger Mouse fleece.

"And I'll come a bit earlier and give you a hand with the stalls until it's our turn to ride," said Chelsea.

"Me too," said Elisha. It was the first time she'd really spoken all evening. "Anita is bringing Darcy for me, but if I can get a lift through earlier, I'll come and help too."

"That's good of you," sniped Emily. JoJo and Chelsea glared at her, but she ignored them.

"Thanks. Some helpers would be great," Amber said, keen to make amends.

She sat quietly in the cab beside Caroline as she drove the horses back to Shaw Farm, thinking about Elisha. The girl had been very quiet. She'd said nothing about the races, just going along with what was decided. She'd made no comment about Amber and Emily's fleeces and the obvious dig that was intended through them. And then she'd offered to help. *Maybe she's changed,* Amber thought, reflecting on how much she'd been dreading Elisha joining their team. *Maybe, now her life isn't so perfect, she won't be such a snob, and she'll be nicer. Maybe Elisha sees that I'm different now. I'm not the timid little girl I was when she met me. Maybe she respects me now.* She smiled at the idea, enjoying the feeling of everything coming together at last.

***

Amber snapped back into the present as she heard JoJo calling to her.

"Amber! You're next to go. Get in position!"

Amber hurriedly kicked Rusty on and took her place on the start line. Emily had just reached the top pole after her second lap of trotting and was flinging herself out of the saddle, ready to run the final stretch and pass the baton to Amber. Running wasn't Emily's forte, but it was Lady's. Hoots of encouragement and good-natured laughter came from the audience as they watched Emily battle to keep up with the racehorse towing her to the finish. By the time Emily reached up to pass the baton to Amber, her face resembled Rudolph's nose.

Amber felt Rusty preparing to surge forward like the other horses. He, too, was expecting a fast getaway. Amber closed her fingers around the reins, and that was enough. Rusty understood what was expected, and instead of charging away in canter, he powered into a ground covering walk. Despite the urgency of the situation,

Amber smiled as she felt the connection to her horse and the way he knew exactly what was going on. They hadn't been in the lead at the changeover, but by the time Amber and Rusty reached the top pole, they were. Rusty didn't break from walk once, or from trot. While their competitors were losing time turning penalty circles, Amber was throwing herself out of the saddle, ready to run to the finish.

"Go on Ammo!"

"Amber, Amber, Amber!" Running alongside Rusty, hearing her name being chanted all around her, Amber beamed. It was so electrifying; she never wanted it to end.

"I can't believe we just did that," said Emily, sliding out of Lady's saddle after the presentation of the horse teams and giving Lady a big hug.

"I can. I told you we'd be an amazing team…again," Amber kissed Rusty on the nose. At one time, she wouldn't have dared to, fearing that she'd lose her own nose to his teeth. But now that Amber knew him better, she knew he was always in a good mood after being ridden. This was the best time to give him affection as he would tolerate it, and today, he was clearly as pleased as she was as he was positively friendly.

Amber acted like she'd known all along that they would win, but her confidence was a show. Secretly it was a massive relief to her that it had gone so well. The Blakefield junior team had only come fourth in their competition, but the senior team: JoJo, Emily, Matty, Ashley and Jake, had won theirs, and the Blakefield horse team had also triumphed. It hadn't looked like it was going to go that way. The atmosphere had been too much for Harris. Amber had expected to get an ear-bashing from Chelsea about how she'd known it wasn't a good idea for a young horse, but she'd surprised everyone at the end by declaring that it had been a good bonding exercise for herself and Harris.

JoJo was delighted with Pluto's performance. He may be super chilled when hacking out, enjoying his horsey daydreams, but he'd proved that he had a competitive spirit and clearly knew the difference between hacking or training in an arena and being at an actual event. Unlike Harris, Pluto loved the electricity of the atmosphere and behaved just like an experienced games pony, whizzing up and down his lane, clearly enjoying racing the other horses and responding to the enthusiastic audience.

"It's just like you said." JoJo was pink-cheeked with exhilaration after winning both her events. "His balance is so much better now, and he's able to move his feet and get them where they need to be miles quicker than before. I think doing this has speeded his brain up, and that can only be a good thing for a cross-country horse!"

Emily was also pleased with Lady's performance, Rusty had been his usual brilliant self in all of his races and Elisha hadn't done or said anything unpleasant. It had been a perfect day. The only thing missing was Caroline.

*I wonder why she didn't come,* Amber wondered, knowing that Emily would have liked her to be there to watch Lady's performance. But she didn't have time to dwell on it. There was still a lot to do before they could head home.

# - Twenty-Two -

# Daylight Robbery

Everything had come together. The Blakefield Blitz was a huge success. Everyone had enjoyed covering their ponies in tinsel, and the festive feeling was enhanced by Christmas tunes being played over the sound system during the breaks between events.

After the presentation of the horse teams, Amber and Emily untacked, rugged and loaded Rusty and Lady back into the trailer where they could munch on hay while the girls went back in to pack up the stalls before heading home. It was just as well the Andersons had replaced their pony trailer with a larger, horse-sized trailer as it had been needed. When Mr Anderson had arrived at the yard earlier, expecting to be travelling to Highland Park in Caroline's lorry with the horses, he'd found that there was a sudden change of plan. One of the lads hadn't turned up to milk the cows that morning, meaning everything was delayed. Caroline had been roped into helping, but they still weren't finished when Mr Anderson arrived at the yard to find her waiting for him.

"I'm really sorry, but I won't be able to take the horses through to Carlisle. I can help you load them in your trailer, and I'll try to follow you through later. I'd really love to watch the girls, but we've got to get these cows milked before they burst." Mr Anderson knew how much she'd hate to let them down like this, but it couldn't be helped. Fortunately, the two horses had loaded into the trailer easily. Rusty had warned Lady off his haynet, but as usual, she ignored him.

"See you later," he called, giving a cheery wave out of the window as he pulled away.

"Yes, hopefully. Tell the girls that I'll definitely try to get through to watch them. I don't want to miss it," Caroline said as she waved back.

But she hadn't made it.

"Wouldn't you think Caroline would have come to watch?" Emily asked as they headed back inside to pack up the stalls. "I mean, she was basically team captain, and I thought she'd have wanted to watch her horse compete."

"She won't have *just not bothered to come.*" Amber stuck up for Caroline, feeling that Emily's real angst was with her own family. Mr Pryde was away with Harry doing something sporty, so her mum had brought her to the event with Pink. But as soon as Emily finished riding in the senior event, her mum had taken the pony home, leaving Emily to get a lift back with the Andersons. Amber knew that she'd have liked her mum and Caroline to be there to cheer her on during the horse event, but she'd had neither. "Something else must've come up at the farm, and she couldn't get away. I know that she really wanted to come. She was looking forward to watching Lady in her Pony Club Games debut!"

Amber mimed jazz hands and earned a slight smile from Emily. The day had gone so well; she didn't want anything to spoil it now. The whole idea had come from wanting to cheer Emily up, so she wasn't allowed to think sad thoughts.

"Let's get tidied up and head back, then you can wave Lady's big red rosette under Caroline's nose. I can't wait to see her face!"

The Andersons, Emily and Georgia worked quickly to pack up the contents of the stalls. There were no cakes left, having all sold out, and all the raffle prizes had been distributed so it didn't take them long to tidy it up and put the boxes into the back of the car.

"The charity thing was such a good idea," said Georgia, who'd enjoyed her day of being unofficially in charge of the stalls when the other girls went off to ride. "Lots of people read the information boards you'd brought about the Brooke, and we raised over £500. Are you going to send it off to them straight away? It'll be a great Christmas present for them. I bet they'll be dead grateful."

"Yes, that's the plan." Amber glowed as they all climbed into the car. "We'll bank it, and Anita's donation, tomorrow and then send them a cheque." The balloon of pride that had been inflating inside her needed to be released and she gave an excited clap of her hands. "Where is the money tin, by the way?"

"It's in here," Mrs Anderson said, opening the glove box. There was a pause as she lifted it out and removed the lid. "What the -?" The sharpness in her voice got everyone's attention, and they all looked at the open tin on Mrs Anderson's lap. "It's gone! Andrew, have you got it? Tell me you've put it in your wallet or something!"

"No, I haven't seen it," Mr Anderson's hand dropped from the car's ignition as he looked into his wife's wide blue eyes. Mrs Anderson turned to the girls in the back seat.

"Georgia, have you seen it, pet? Have you put it somewhere different? To keep it safe?"

"N…o…." Georgia's reply came in slow motion as if she couldn't believe what was happening.

"Oh…no, no, no!" Mrs Anderson scrabbled around in the obviously empty glove box, as if she hoped the money had somehow climbed out of the tin and was hiding in one of the dark corners. "I only left it for a minute while I went to the toilet. I didn't lock the car in case Dad or Georgia wanted in for something. I…."

"You didn't lock…?" Amber started but held the rest of the words back. Her mother hadn't done this on purpose. She hadn't lost the money. Somebody must have seen her putting the red biscuit tin they'd been using for the takings in the car and rushing off without locking it. It would only have taken them seconds to open the car, then the glove box, remove the tin's lid and take the money.

The notes had all been held together with an elastic band and would have been easy to snatch, but they'd even scooped out all the loose change too. That would have taken longer and been more difficult to do. They hadn't left a single penny behind. Whoever had taken it must have been desperate…desperate enough to want every last coin and to take the time to get it all and risk being seen. Who could that be?

"Elisha!" she said out loud just as the idea popped into her head. "It'll be Elisha who'll have taken it. Who needs money more than her now she's got none? I bet that was the reason why she suddenly wanted to be on the team, out of nowhere: she knew we were doing this charity thing, and it was a perfect opportunity for her to have a reason to be here so she could get her hands on it. And she even offered to help!"

"Amber, you can't just accuse someone," Mrs Anderson reprimanded her, her eyes slightly blurry as she continued to stare into the empty tin. "There were so many people around today; it could've been anyone. And Elisha was lovely when she helped with the stalls. I'm sorry, love. You've worked so hard on this, and it's my fault. Why didn't I lock the car?"

"It's not your fault Mum, it's Elisha's; I know it. She's not lovely. Ever. And she had a good reason to want to do this to me, besides the money." She locked eyes with Emily, remembering Elisha's face when she'd seen Amber wearing her Thundercat fleece at the arena practice. "Revenge."

Emily blinked rapidly, and her face tightened as if she was preparing for battle. "Are you blaming me for this?"

"Well, I don't think the stunt with the fleeces will have helped, do you?"

"You don't even know it was definitely her who took it."

"Oh, you're sticking up for her now, are you?"

"Girls! Stop it. There's no need for you to fall out about it. What a rotten end to a wonderful day. I just can't believe anyone would steal from a charity event organised single-handedly by a child...and at Christmas too," Mrs Anderson said, coming to Georgia's rescue. The young girl was sandwiched between Amber and Emily on the back seat and had put her hands over her ears as their bickering began to escalate.

The journey home was silent. Amber and Emily were plugged into their phones and didn't utter a word until they arrived back at the farmyard. Amber wondered what Emily was thinking. It was the first time they'd ever had cross words, and her stomach felt like it was eating itself from the inside out. She messaged JoJo and Chelsea to fill them in and share her suspicion of Elisha. They were predictably outraged by the theft of the charity takings and irritatingly unwilling to take her side over her accusation of Elisha.

As they pulled in to the farm yard, it was almost dark. The farm dogs, Tess and Kelly came out to bark at them until they realised who they were, then they slunk off, back to their beds in one of the outbuildings. Amber lowered the trailer's front ramp and led Lady out, while Georgia appointed herself as Rusty's groom. The horse had been gradually getting used to her presence, since she'd taken on the role of child-proofing the grumpy horse. He now tolerated her with only mild head shakes and wrinkled nostrils, which Georgia took as excellent progress.

“Look, he likes me now,” she often told Amber when she entered his stable, and he no longer showed his teeth.

Grateful to be away from the atmosphere in the car, Georgia could be heard chattering away to Rusty as she led him into his stable. Amber and Emily worked in silence to remove Lady’s boots and bandages and swap her travel rug for a stable rug. Emily gave her hay while Amber got the feed they’d prepared earlier. Having finished attending to Rusty, Georgia was now helping Mrs Anderson quickly check on the Fell ponies in the field while Mr Anderson unhitched the trailer and mucked it out. Everything still needed to be unloaded from the car and put away.

“Sorry,” Amber looked at the stone flags of the stable floor as she spoke. “It wasn’t really fair…what I said earlier.”

“No, it was,” Emily sighed. “I shouldn’t have done that with the fleeces. If Elisha did steal the money, that might have been part of the reason. She won’t have known that it was my idea. She must’ve thought it was down to you and wanted to punish you for it. I’m really sorry. After all that work you put in. It’s awful.”

A sob that Amber hadn't known was there burst from her before she could stop it.

"I knew it was too good to be true. Everything was going so well. Do you know, some members from the other horse teams even found me at the end and thanked me for organising it? They said it was great to play games with their horses, and they would never have thought of it. And we won…and we raised all that money…it was just a perfect day. And it has to end like this. Why?"

Tears pushed their way out as Emily pulled her into a hug. "I know," she said simply.

Later that evening, after a takeaway tea and a bath, the hollowness in Amber's stomach refused to budge. The joy and achievement from the day should have filled her up like a hot-air balloon for at least the rest of the week, but she was empty. At least she'd made things up with Emily. That was the only good thing. The fact that Caroline hadn't come out of the house to see how they'd got on also upset her. Didn't she care? It was pitch black when they left the yard, and there had been no lights on in the farmhouse. It looked like everyone was out. Amber frowned. Not only had Caroline failed to come to the event to watch as she'd said she would, she wasn't even in to welcome them back and ask how they'd done. It wasn't like her. She'd been so excited about it – the most excited Amber had ever seen her, anyway.

The news blared on the TV. Amber wasn't paying much attention. She had Stig the cat in her lap and was concentrating on the smooth gloss of his sleek black fur as she stroked him. But as the local news came on, the opening story made her look up.

"Our first story tonight is about a car accident that occurred today around lunchtime on the A595 south of Carlisle. Two motorists were involved in a head-on collision." The screen showed the wreckage of the cars. They were badly deformed with twisted metal and shattered glass making them unrecognisable. Except for the number plate of the silver car which was visible. Amber gasped when she read the registration. "A twenty-three-year-old woman and a nineteen-year-old man were the only passengers in the two cars and are now being treated in hospital. The woman is described as being in a critical condition. Police are appealing for witnesses. If anyone saw the accident involving a silver Peugeot and red BMW, you are asked to contact Cumbria Police on

101 to give details. Next, we move to Penrith where James Logan brings us a story about some rather friendly reindeer..."

The three members of the Anderson family sat like stone statues for a moment, taking in what they'd just seen and heard. The silver Peugeot was Caroline's car. For all of them, the memory of driving past a POLICE ACCIDENT sign on the way back from Highland Park jumped into their mind. Tired and upset from their long day and its outcome, they'd paid little attention to it.

Mrs Anderson's phone pinged with a message. Then another and another. With a shaking hand, she swiped the screen and read the messages there.

"It's from Lou, JoJo's mum. She says Caroline has been airlifted to Newcastle. They're doing scans on her. She's unconscious. The man who crashed into her…is *Troy Templeton*. He's not badly hurt."

"Troy Templeton…you know who that must be?" Mr Anderson said.

"What does 'critical condition' mean?" Amber asked, her voice trembling as her mind fixed on the phrase the news reader had used. "Caroline's going skiing on Tuesday," she added, unable to comprehend the meaning of the words whizzing around her brain, making her feel dizzy.

The unanswered questions hung in the air like storm clouds threatening to burst.

"That means..." Amber started in a whisper, the sudden dryness of her throat catching on her words, "she was on her way. She was coming to watch us, just like she promised." Amber's nose prickled painfully as hot tears rushed into her eyes. They fell, burning tracks over her cheeks as they flowed, like the tyre tracks she imagined would be scorched into the road. Caroline's tracks.

Stig felt the howl forming itself deep within Amber's core and leapt out of her lap before it ripped its way out of her. It was a sound Amber had never heard before. It was pain and rage and hurt and regret and guilt, and it came from an ache deep inside her that was unbearable.

Her parents were there, arms around her in an instant, as if they could shield her from the anguish. But they couldn't. What had happened couldn't be undone. The multi-coloured lights on the Christmas tree swam and blurred into a vision of flashing blue bulbs from police cars and ambulances, and the glare of flames, flickering orange and red.

Just hours ago, she'd been laughing with her teammates, enjoying a shared experience and a sense of achievement. Then the money had been stolen, and the day's joy had tilted and slipped away like a sinking ship. It had felt like the end of the world, but now Amber would give anything for some stolen money to be the worst of her problems. The police had been informed – maybe they would sort it out. But never mind the money. If only the lad who was supposed to be milking that morning had turned up, Caroline would have been with them, instead of on that road hours later. If only Caroline hadn't brought Rusty to her. If only her new horse hadn't been an overgrown games pony. If only Amber hadn't organised the horse event at the Blakefield Blitz. If only Caroline hadn't let Emily borrow Lady for it... *Noooooo! You can't blame Caroline for any of this,* the voice in her head screamed at her.

*I know that,* she bawled back at it. *It's not Caroline's fault...it's MINE!*

*No,* said the voice that occasionally came to her rescue. *There's someone you're forgetting...Troy Templeton.*

*Templeton...Elisha! This is something to do with her. I know it is.*

Amber turned all her fear and fury towards Elisha. She hadn't changed at all. Amber had been stupid and naïve to think so. Yes, it was her brother driving the car that crashed into Caroline, but Elisha would be connected to it somehow; she just knew it. And she'd find a way to prove it too.

She had to.

For Caroline.

# Author's Note

What can I say about my little Rustbucket? How I loved this horse! I don't want to say too much as there's still one more APT story to come, but I will say that he was very special to me.

Rusty was a grumpy so-and-so in the stable all his life. He never grew out of his protectiveness over food and always hated having rugs on and his girth done up. But outside of the stable, he was just wonderful, and riding him was a brilliant way to put myself in a good mood. He was always so enthusiastic and gung-ho when ridden, even if it was just a hack out, that being with him instantly lifted the spirits! I found this a great help during my teenage years (I was fourteen when I got Rusty) and beyond as he stayed with me for the rest of his life.

Although he could be moody, he and I were a brilliant match (maybe because I was a moody teenager myself), and he quickly restored all the confidence I lost with Molly through our being mismatched. With Rusty, I could do anything, and it made me believe in myself. He wasn't big or impressive or well-bred, but together, we were a force. Just a little force, but it was a start!

We believed Rusty to be at least part thoroughbred, and he had a very competitive streak. He always wanted to beat any other horse he was ridden out with and made everything into a race, even if it was just walking. He had to have his head in front and would battle to win any gallops, no matter who the competition was. If he had been a full thoroughbred, he'd have been a fantastic racehorse as he had a proper will to win.

Rusty really did love mounted games, and we often did the senior games at gymkhanas and in trophy shows where he was usually the winner. He was never ever beaten in his favourite game – walk, trot and lead', and its mate, walk, trot and gallop. Although the Blakefield Blitz is made up, my Pony Club did run a similar competition for local clubs every year, and at least once, they had a 'senior' competition for those riders who were fifteen and over and therefore too old for Pony Club Games teams. You didn't have to be on a horse, and most people weren't since most horses aren't great at games, but I was on my club's team with Rusty. He was every bit as good as the ponies.

Rusty was fun, fast and feisty. I never knew a moment's fear with him and thought of him as completely safe. This was proved to be incorrect, though, as he took off with everyone else who rode him over the years when I let friends ride him. I thought he was completely trustworthy, though, and I still think of him and miss him, even now.

# Acknowledgements

As always, there are plenty of people to thank for their involvement with this book. Firstly, thanks to Carol Elliot, Alex Connors, Julie Page, Emma Whitaker, Nicola and Lydia Cooper, for advice and information on the sport of tetrathlon at championship level. Robert Scott helped to answer my questions about Mounted Games as it's been a long time since I did them! Bekah Hocking was my advisor for queries about 'Young Farmers.' Thank you!

My pre-publication team were invaluable for their feedback on the manuscript: Emily, Caitlyn, Kim, Helen, Lizzie, Grace and Zara, I really appreciate your support.

The pony on the cover representing Rusty is Flash, AKA Matley Sparkey, who was entered by his owner Tally McGowan in the Cover Star competition for this book. The picture of Flash was taken by Marlyn McInnes and the background by Neil Routledge. Thank you to all of them for their involvement as well as Amanda Horan at Let's Get Booked for producing the final cover design. Thanks to Amanda, too, for editing and formatting the manuscript. She's been with me all the way on Amber's adventures since Book 1. Neither of us are looking forward to working on the next Amber's Pony Tales story as it will be the last. We've enjoyed working together on this series.

Thanks to The Brooke, who gave permission for me to use them as Amber's charity in this book. They're a fantastic charity, supporting welfare for working animals in the world's poorest countries. Working horses, donkeys and mules are critical to their owners' livelihoods and The Brooke's work promotes a culture of care for animals and humans. To find out more about what they do and where the work, visit

https://www.thebrooke.org/

Final thanks go to Mel Avery and my husband, Martyn, for proofreading the manuscript. Their attention to detail is a great help in getting the story publication ready.

For free bonus material linked to this book, plus news, competitions, and exclusive opportunities connected to the author's other books, sign up to the mailing list at www.helenharaldsen.co.uk

Coming soon: Book 6.
What's in store for Amber in the final book of the series?

*Follow Amber's Pony Tales on Facebook.*

Printed in Great Britain
by Amazon